# SLEEPING BEAUTY

On impulse, Lord Norwich stopped by Allie's room before his departure for the theater. He wanted to assure himself that she had everything she needed. When there was no answer to his soft knock, he opened the door. It was dark in the room except for a shaft of early moonlight streaming through the window. He should leave at once, he knew, but something drew him to the big bed. Pulling back the bed curtains, he stood staring down at the young woman newly come into his life.

Her brown hair was plaited down her back, her dark lashes shadowing her cheeks. Involuntarily, he reached out to caress that cheek. She was pretty, even thin as she was, and something about her gentle nature clutched at his heart.

Stepping back from temptation, he left the room. She was a member of his family and under his protection. She was also, he reminded himself, an accused murderess . . .

# THE
# NOTORIOUS
# WIDOW

## Judy Christenberry

PAGEANT BOOKS

PAGEANT BOOKS
225 Park Avenue South
New York, New York 10003

Cover artwork by Ray Yeldman

Printed in the U.S.A.

First Pageant Books printing: October, 1988

10 9 8 7 6 5 4 3 2 1

*For Laura, Christina, and Faye;*
*and in memory of George*

# THE
# NOTORIOUS
# WIDOW

# Chapter One

A tall gentleman exquisitely dressed in a blue superfine coat abruptly drew a snowy linen handkerchief from his inside pocket and held it to his nose. Though his journeys had led him from Egypt to Cathay, the stench of London's most notorious prison was worse than any he had previously encountered.

"That be 'er, me lord," the rough voice of his guide growled, grating on the gentleman's already strained sensibilities. His eyes searched in the dim light among the group of women in the small cell, staring at him from behind the grate, their eyes showing no emotion save fear. They were all dirty, starved, and silent. He realized he had no way of recognizing the woman he sought.

After a brief glance at the burly guard, the man moved forward a step and inquired in a pleasant voice, "Mrs. Montgomery?"

There was no movement, just blank stares, until a fairly young woman, blond, he thought, though it was difficult to see, stepped forward. "What do you want with her?"

"Out o' the way, Mav," the guard said roughly.

It took only a look from the gentleman to stir the guard into acting on the gentleman's behalf in spite of the jade's angry posture. "Aw right, lady. Come on over 'ere and let the gent 'ave a look at ye." The threat implicit in his tone caused a stir among the prisoners and a young woman was pushed forward from their midst with several jabs from her neighbors, none of whom wanted to anger their jailer.

The Earl of Norwich stared at the frail young woman who stood behind the grate. This was his brother's widow. Her eyes lowered to the floor, the fragile figure was unresponsive. The gown she was wearing had seen better days, and her long chestnut hair was untidily plaited.

"You are Mrs. Montgomery, widow of Edward Montgomery?"

She made no move toward acknowledgment.

The guard pushed his stick through the bars and just missed the woman's right shoulder. "Answer 'im!"

"Enough!" the Earl of Norwich shouted as the blond woman leapt up to shield the fragile victim from further assault.

"I didn't mean no 'arm, me lord," the burly man whined, his harshness tempered by the now fierce look on the nobleman's face.

Ignoring the guard's feeble apology, he demanded, "Release the woman at once."

"I can't do that, me lord, wi'out . . ."

"Here are the papers," the Earl snapped, thrusting them at the man with distaste.

The guard gingerly reached for the document. He studied it laboriously as the gentleman watched him, though his eyes returned to observe the pathetic figure crumpled against the side wall, now almost totally supported by the blond woman.

With great reluctance, the guard withdrew a large ring of keys from his pocket and unlocked the heavy door. Pushing it open, the guard looked from his charges to the tall man standing in the hallway. "Com' on, now. The gent 'ere wants to take ye 'ome wi' 'im."

Instead of the rush to freedom both men expected, the young prisoner surprised them by drawing back and clinging to the blond woman beside her. The guard looked at the gentleman next to him, afraid to offer any more assistance.

The Earl spoke softly. "Mrs. Montgomery, you have nothing to fear. Mr. Browning has told me all about you." At the mention of his man of business, both young women turned toward him, the blonde moving closer while still supporting Mrs. Montgomery.

"Mr. Browning sent you?" she shot back. "Have you got proof?"

"Proof? My dear woman, I am the Earl of Norwich."

"How do we know we can believe you?" Heads nodded in the darkness approving her caution.

This was hardly the reaction the Earl expected.

However, he silently extended his hand to the guard and the man returned the piece of paper he had earlier perused. "Can you read?" he asked the blonde.

"Mrs. Montgomery will read it," the young woman answered, taking the paper and handing it to her silent friend. After examining the paper, Mrs. Montgomery raised her gaze to study the waiting man. It was the first time he received a view of her face, and her large brown eyes were shadowed with pain.

"Are you quite satisfied that I am the Earl of Norwich?" he asked in a tone tinged with sarcasm.

Mrs. Montgomery stepped forward and spoke for the first time in a husky but melodious voice. "Yes, my lord, but . . . but I cannot leave this— this place without Mavis."

"Aw, no, that paper don't say nothin' 'bout 'er leavin'," the guard protested.

"I assume you are Mavis?" Lord Norwich's voice reminded the guard of his rank. "And are you a murderess too?"

"A thief, my lord. That's what they say. But I'm no more a thief than she's a murderer."

Mrs. Montgomery appealed to the Earl. "Please, you can't know what it's like here. That guard will hurt her as soon as I'm gone. He's only held off because of Mr. Browning. If I go . . . please, she has saved my life. I cannot leave her here."

"Do you have a last name?" the Earl quietly asked the other woman, ignoring his sister-in-law's plea.

"Thompson, my lord. Mavis Thompson."

"I will return as soon as possible with the proper papers, ladies." He turned from their surprised faces and addressed the seething guard. "If you lay so much as a finger on either of those two ladies in my absence, you will not survive long enough to hang."

There was no doubt the guard believed him, as he led the gentleman from the environs of Newgate.

Mr. Timothy Browning had already risen from his desk by the time Norwich passed through the outer office to reach his door. His eyes eagerly scanned the tanned face, but he found no answers save an angry frown.

"You have her safe?"

"No!" the Earl snapped.

"But what went wrong? You had the papers, there should have been no difficulty."

"She refused to come."

"What?" Mr. Browning stared at his employer as the Earl paced up and down the room.

"How can a civilized society treat females like that, particularly one as gently bred as Mrs. Montgomery? My animals are better housed and treated than those women!"

"I know, my lord."

"How could you allow them to place her there?"

Timothy Browning heaved a sigh. When he reviewed the past two months and took stock of his almost ceaseless activity on behalf of Mrs. Montgomery, he was tempted to hurl the nearest object at his questioner. But since Mrs. Montgomery was merely a merchant's daughter, not born into the Polite World, in spite of her marriage, he had had little hope of obtaining her release, or even gaining many concessions. Her wealthy father, who might have been able to assist her, had died of shock when told of her arrest. After all, Mrs. Montgomery was accused of killing her husband.

On his own, all Mr. Browning had managed was the right to visit as often as he wished and a delay of the trial until the Earl's return. In the interim he had traveled each day to Newgate prison to bring food and hope to the hapless prisoner. Only the Earl, brother of the deceased, crony of the Prince, could possibly save Mrs. Montgomery from the gallows. And now the Earl wanted to know how Browning could have allowed such a thing to happen!

"I did my best, my lord. Perhaps if I were to go to Newgate, Mrs. Montgomery would leave with me."

"Not unless you can obtain the release of a wench named Mavis Thompson."

Mr. Browning's eyes narrowed. "I should have known."

"What should you have known?"

"I had thought to go to the prison after you freed Mrs. Montgomery and obtain Miss Thompson's release. Both Mrs. Montgomery and I have reason to be grateful to her. But I should have realized Mrs. Montgomery wouldn't leave without her."

"What will it take to have this Miss Thompson released?"

"Merely the price of a diamond ring. I could have had her released weeks ago. Mrs. Montgomery asked me to do so, but Mavis . . . I mean, Miss Thompson, refused to leave your sister-in-law alone there. She is a very headstrong young woman."

"A kind thief, then?" Lord Norwich was surprised at the anger that sprang into Mr. Browning's expression.

"No thief at all, my lord. Her employer, a lady of fashion, accused her of theft to get rid of her. Mavis never had a chance! Yet, I suspect some foul play on the part of a male member of that household. And jealousy on the part of some of the females."

Lord Norwich shook his head and asked without further comment, "How soon can we get them out of there?"

"Possibly this afternoon or first thing in the morning. I have the papers from Miss Thompson's case in my file."

"Get them! I would prefer that Mrs. Montgomery not spend another night in that place."

"Then you believe she's innocent?"

"I don't know what I believe!" He paused. "But we both know she had just cause to do injury to Edward, if indeed she did. And whether guilty or not, I will not have a member of my family incarcerated in such a hell."

"No, my lord," Mr. Browning agreed quietly, handing over the papers for Mavis.

"When I return to Newgate, I would prefer that you accompany me. I believe Mrs. Montgomery is loath to trust me."

Lord Norwich stared into the fire flickering in the grate, his thoughts on the events of the day. He had never before been inside Newgate. He found it disturbing. It was inconceivable to him that his England could treat anyone, even convicts, in that manner.

That his own sister-in-law should be incarcerated there was beyond his comprehension. When he had first looked into that dark, filthy dungeon and seen the frail figure of his brother's widow, gazed upon her fragile features, he had been amazed that she had survived.

Since bringing her home that morning, his butler reported she had bathed, eaten a light meal, and slept the day away, after being checked by the doctor. The doctor's report had indicated it would be several weeks before the young lady or her companion would regain their complete strength, but he felt sure no lasting damage had been done.

Except perhaps that done by his brother. Lord Norwich knew little about his brother's marriage. He had only learned of it when Browning's urgent message arrived in Rome, requesting his immediate return to England for the trial of his sister-in-law. Mr. Browning had also informed him of his brother's death, knowing, perhaps, it would not be a great blow. They had never been close.

Lord Norwich had been eight years old when

his father had remarried and immediately produced a second son, Edward. His young stepmother had resented the fact that her son was not the heir and had done all she could to prejudice her husband in her son's favor. Her son had grown up spoiled and resentful, a thoughtless, selfish, insensitive young man.

According to the few words Lord Norwich exchanged with his solicitor before obtaining the release of his sister-in-law, his brother had not varied from his previous pattern of behavior.

That Edward had married the woman for her fortune was evident. The former Miss Allison Tipton, while she came from good yeoman stock, was hardly a suitable bride for an aristocrat.

Mr. Browning had told him of the marriage settlement given by her father, generous by any standards, and of the intention his brother had voiced, immediately prior to his murder, of divorcing his wife since the financial benefits of his marriage were finally in his hands. Under the circumstances, even if his sister-in-law had ended his brother's life, she had rid London of an infamous libertine.

His butler interrupted his musing. "My lord, Mr. Browning has arrived."

"Send him in, Jeffers. We will dine in half an hour."

"Very good, my lord."

His man of business had returned to his office, promising to join him for dinner later that evening in order to clear up some of the mysteries surrounding his brother's death.

"Lord Norwich."

"Come in, Browning."

"How are Mrs. Montgomery and Mavis? Are they recovering from their ordeal?"

"According to Dr. Wainwright, they will recover in time, perhaps two weeks, with no lasting damage. Would you care for a drink?" he offered, gesturing to the bottle of sherry on a silver tray.

"Yes, thank you."

After pouring, Lord Norwich handed the drink to his guest and resumed his seat, a frown creasing his brow.

"I don't really know where to begin with my questions. I assume Edward married the chit for her fortune?" A brief nod was Mr. Browning's only response. "And I assume the marriage contract was drawn up by you?" He was surprised when Mr. Browning denied such activity.

"But you are . . . were my brother's solicitor."

"Yes, my lord, but he feared I might insist that the agreement be fair to both parties."

Lord Norwich studied the man before him as their eyes met. About ten years older than Lord Norwich's own thirty years, Mr. Browning's blond hair scarcely showed the gray that was beginning to dominate his sideburns. His figure was tall and muscular, his mien pleasant.

It was his gray eyes, however, that informed the observer that Mr. Browning would not be easily hoodwinked. Lord Norwich could understand his brother avoiding any revelation of his plan to the upright gentleman opposite him. "But you did see the agreement?"

"Only after both parties had signed it. Your

brother gave it to me to process the transfer of ownership of the funds and various properties."

"And did you follow his instructions?"

"Of course, my lord."

"So the entire settlement had been transferred to my brother at the time of his death?"

"Yes, my lord."

"What happens to his estate now?"

"If Mrs. Montgomery is found guilty, she goes to the gallows and the estate will come to you. If not, she inherits."

"I see." Lord Norwich studied Browning, who neither moved nor dropped his eyes. "And you are of the opinion my sister-in-law is innocent?"

"Yes, my lord."

"Why?"

Mr. Browning answered calmly. "Her appearance alone would convince any man of her innocence."

Lord Norwich leaned back in his chair, his eyelids drooping. "But, Browning, appearances can be greatly deceiving. My brother seemed the perfect gentleman, but we both know the opposite was true."

"Agreed, my lord. However, in size and strength alone, it would be difficult for Mrs. Montgomery to wield the murder weapon effectively."

The remembrance of the slight figure he met in the prison confirmed that statement, but the Earl persisted, "She was not more robust at the time of their marriage?"

"Of course, Lord Norwich, but even so . . ."

"But if my brother were asleep . . ."

"Which is possible. There was no sign of a struggle."

"Then she could have killed him."

Mr. Browning's lips tightened, but he refrained from answering, only nodding in response.

"And if, as you have discovered, he intended to divorce her once he gained control of her fortune, she had a motive."

"More than enough motive, my lord," Mr. Browning agreed grimly.

"Is there more than the divorce, Browning?"

"Only speculation on my part, my lord. I know Mrs. Montgomery seldom left the house, had no visitors, and it was not widely known that your brother had married. Only a few of his cronies were aware of his wife's existence."

Before Lord Norwich could ask for more details, Jeffers announced dinner and the two men adjourned to the dining room. In the presence of the servants, Lord Norwich chose to satisfy his appetite rather than his curiosity.

Allie lay uneasily beneath the thick comforter. After two months in Newgate, the softness of her bed, the sensation of a full stomach, the joy of a hot bath, were welcome. Her situation had changed so dramatically in only hours. But why had Lord Norwich had her freed?

Fear caused Allie to shiver beneath the covers. Could there be any similarity between the brothers? Perhaps Lord Norwich wanted revenge. The only reassurance she had was Mr. Browning's presence. She knew he would not lend himself to any such scheme. Whatever Lord Norwich's reasons for obtaining her release, she was grateful for her comfortable situation this night.

Sleep was creeping upon her. Her last thought before it overtook her was the wish for Mavis's presence . . .

## Chapter Two

Lord Norwich hurried Mr. Browning through his dinner in order to return to the drawing room where they would be uninterrupted. He hoped to learn more details of his brother's murder. He also wondered if Mr. Browning had a second suspect in mind since he was so convinced of Mrs. Montgomery's innocence.

As he was ushering his guest back across the wide hall, heels echoing against the marble floor, their progress was halted by a piercing scream that rang through the great house.

Lord Norwich did not wait for his butler to act. He had no time for the elderly man's stately ascent to the second floor. As he dashed up the stairs, Mr. Browning hesitated only a moment before following. His devotion to Mrs. Montgomery had grown in the past two months, changing from pity to concern and admiration for withstanding what might have killed a weaker woman. He could not let the fact that he was a guest in Lord Norwich's house deter him from offering his assistance to Mrs. Montgomery or to Mavis.

When the two men arrived at the chamber where Mrs. Montgomery had been installed, the door was standing open and, entering without further ado, they found several housemaids and the housekeeper surrounding the bed as they tried to soothe the distraught young widow.

Before Lord Norwich could even question the circumstances, he was pushed aside by the arrival of Mavis Thompson. The young woman went directly to the bed and took Mrs. Montgomery's hands into hers. "What's to do?"

"Mavis! I . . . I had a terrible dream! We were back in Newgate with that guard, and I awoke and you were gone and . . ."

"I'm here now. It's all right," she said in a tender voice as she sat on the side of the bed, her arm around the shivering figure huddled in the tumbled bedclothes.

Lord Norwich dismissed the gaping servants, unhappy that they had seen the familiarity between Mavis and Mrs. Montgomery.

After their departure, he said, "Madam, I realize what you have been through, but if you are not careful your lack of decorum will cause difficulties." If Mr. Browning believed that Lord Norwich was being unduly harsh, he kept silent.

The recipient of his warning, however, ignored him entirely and, after one blank look, turned to Mavis. "Could you not stay in here with me tonight, Mavis?"

The girl glanced at Lord Norwich's rigid features and replied carefully, "I'm afraid I can't, ma'am. They gave me a room on the top floor."

Allie's eyes searched her friend's face. "There is no need to address me formally, Mavis. We are friends, are we not?"

The young woman made no attempt to answer, gesturing slightly toward her host before looking appealingly to her friend.

"Ah, I see," Allie said. "You must understand, Mavis, that what occurs between you and me has nothing to do with his lordship." With a challenging look at the silent man, she continued, "Without you, I would not have survived. The debt I owe you transcends society's conventions, as does the debt I owe you, Lord Norwich and Mr. Browning, which is why I excuse the impropriety of your presence in my room."

When Allie realized how inappropriate her imperious tones were in the circumstances, her cheeks burned, and she added, "My apologies, my lord. You surely have exceeded the bounds of generosity by rescuing your brother's accused murderer. I am in your debt."

Lord Norwich responded in even tones. "No apology is necessary."

There was an awkward pause before Lord Norwich continued. "Would you care to return to your rest? I will see to it that a bed is prepared here for Mavis, if that is your wish."

Allie now felt even guiltier for her reaction. "Thank you, my lord, that will be . . . No, no, I do not want to rest. I mean, I do, but I must know why you brought me here and what you intend to do with me." Only the slightest quiver in her final words revealed Allie's fears.

Lord Norwich studied the frail figure sitting up stiffly in her bed. "Perhaps you are right, Mrs. Montgomery. I believe it would be better to talk now about what has happened so that you may take full advantage of your rest when next you take to your bed. Would you . . . and . . . Miss Thompson care to join us in my library?"

Mrs. Montgomery did not hesitate. "Thank you, my lord. We will come down as soon as we have dressed."

The two men descended the stairs in silence, Lord Norwich speaking only when faced with his butler's waiting figure. "Ah, Jeffers, the two . . . ladies will be joining Mr. Browning and myself in the library. Have Cook prepare a tea tray. And then we do not want to be disturbed."

"Very good, my lord."

Mr. Browning watched Lord Norwich pace the library floor as they waited for the ladies. "What *do* you have planned for Mrs. Montgomery?" he asked curiously.

"Damn it, Browning, how would I know? A month ago I did not even know of her existence!" Lord Norwich frowned as he saw his solicitor stiffen, his face now void of all emotion.

"Of course, my lord."

"Are you going to cut up stiff every time I am frustrated, Browning? If so, you are in for a difficult evening." The slight smile that acompanied his words provoked a similar response in the other man.

"I had not thought myself to be so prickly, my

lord. I suppose it is the concern I feel for the ladies' future."

The frown returned to Lord Norwich's face as their conversation was halted by the entrance of the two women. The cause of his displeasure was not their presence, however, but the state of their attire.

"Mrs. Montgomery, have you nothing more . . . more attractive than that gown?"

Allie looked at her brother-in-law in bewilderment, then down at the dove-gray gown, hanging loosely on her thin frame. "I am sorry, my lord. I will return to my room and dress in my Sunday best. It is the only dress that is more modish than these," she answered, gesturing to both her own dress and the almost identical one loaned to Mavis.

"But I had your belongings brought from my brother's town house this afternoon while you rested. That dratted maid must have slipped out instead of hanging your gowns. I'll have her head for this!" he raged, venting his edginess on the unsuspecting servant.

"No, my lord! All my clothes were hanging in the wardrobe, freshly pressed. It—it was very thoughtful of you to . . ."

"What of your brideclothes?" At her uncomprehending stare, he tried again. "Your trousseau?"

Allie's fingers tightened against the skirt of her gown before she consciously smoothed them out. "There was no time for such finery, my lord. I will return to my room. We will have our discussion at another time when you are more . . ."

Before she could find the appropriate word to describe her host's mood, Jeffers knocked on the closed doors to announce the arrival of the tea tray.

The footmen following Jeffers advanced to the small table in front of the sofa, lowering two trays, one carrying the tea and the second filled with mouth-watering delicacies for which Lord Norwich's cook was justly famous. Mavis's eyes grew round in wonder as she stared at the offerings and even Mrs. Montgomery was distracted from her intention to depart by the munificence of the Earl's tea.

Mr. Browning, an interested observer of the proceedings, grinned at their reactions. Catching the impatient Earl's eye, he silently motioned to the refreshments. With a nod and a smile of thanks, Lord Norwich placed a hand on each lady's arm and escorted them to the gilded sofa. "If you ladies will serve tea, I believe we should all refresh ourselves."

Mrs. Montgomery asked, "You want us to stay, my lord?"

"Of course. I did not mean to imply that I found your appearance distasteful. I was merely concerned that my servants might not have carried out my orders."

Mr. Browning's eyes gleamed with appreciation for Lord Norwich's tact as he settled into the wing chair near the sofa. Lord Norwich seated himself across the small table from the women and waited expectantly.

"Shall I serve?" Allie asked.

"Yes, please."

Mavis's eyes swung back and forth between the two speakers, her unease growing. Then she rose to her feet. "I better wait upstairs."

Allie put down the ornately carved silver teapot she had just picked up to turn and stare at her friend. "Mavis, what . . ."

"I'm not suited to tea in the parlor," she whispered, all the time edging away from the other three.

"Mavis, be seated!" Lord Norwich's stern voice of authority ordered and Mavis responded to it without conscious thought.

"Now," he continued in a more ordinary tone of voice, "you must understand, Mavis. Mrs. Montgomery needs your support while we discuss her difficult circumstances."

"Yes, my lord," Mavis agreed in a small voice.

Allie resumed her duties as hostess, filling the first cup and looking askance at Lord Norwich. He nodded imperceptibly at her companion and Allie offered the cup to Mavis.

"N-no, I . . ." A cool stare from the master of the house found Mavis swallowing her protest and receiving the delicate cup and saucer into her work-worn hands. She waited while the others received their tea, watching with gritted teeth as Lord Norwich casually reached over to the other tray of small cakes and served himself several.

She could not know the man was wondering how he would possibly find room for even such delicacies as these when he had just arisen from the dinner table. But it behooved him to put the women at their ease.

Allie, well trained in polite behavior by her

maiden aunt, with whom she had lived most of her life, was aware of her friend's discomfort and silently touched her hand, indicating Mavis should follow her lead. It was a procedure already employed in the prison, Allie using the time that crept by so slowly to help Mavis with the rudiments of reading.

Both men watched closely under cover of the social chatter as the two women gradually relaxed. There was admiration in their eyes as Mavis even went so far as to nibble on a small piece of cake.

Lord Norwich also watched his sister-in-law, remembering how many women in society did a good deed only to prate on about it endlessly. Mrs. Montgomery gave no indication anything out of the ordinary had occurred.

When both ladies seemed to have had their fill of the delicacies urged on them by Lord Norwich's gentle teasing, he rang for the trays to be removed, sitting back down only after the servants had left the room.

"Now, madam, I would like you to tell me how you met my brother and why the two of you were married."

Allie had dreaded this moment. To explain the events of the past few months seemed a task beyond her capabilities, but the blue eyes staring at her across the tea table left no room for retreat.

"I met Mr. Montgomery on the day of our wedding."

Lord Norwich waited for her to continue, but as the silence grew, he prompted her. "Perhaps I should rephrase my question. How did the marriage come about?"

"I do not know how your brother met my father. Papa was a businessman in the city. I do not even know exactly what kinds of business he operated, but he was wildly successful. At least, that is what my aunt told me. I had not seen him for three years. And before that visit, which lasted only two days, he had not come to see me since I was seven."

"You did not live with your father?"

"No, my lord. My mother died in childbirth when I was four and my father knew nothing of raising children. He sent me to live with my aunt in Birmingham." Allie's eyes drifted to the deep green velvet hangings at the window as she thought back to being a frightened child, bereft with grief over her mother's death. How her care was thrust upon the mercies of a stern maiden aunt who lived in what Allie thought was a strange little house.

"And your aunt raised you?"

"Yes, because my father paid her twelve pounds a year and she had little income from her needlework."

The bare-bones statement was no plea for pity, but it evoked a fellow feeling in Lord Norwich as he remembered the arrival of his new stepmother, finding himself, at the age of eight, almost completely shut out of his father's life. It seemed he had more in common with this new member of his family than he had realized.

"How did you learn of your engagement?" he probed.

"My father arrived one day without warning, excited and happy. He told me he had arranged a bright future for me, that it was time I be of some benefit to him, since I had not been the son he wanted . . ."

Allie stopped abruptly as she realized what she had admitted.

"I . . . it was my duty to do as my father requested. I packed my things at once. I even began to daydream of my future husband, and going to parties, the London Season."

Her chin rose as she looked at Lord Norwich. "I know that sounds shallow, my lord, but my aunt was isolated from the villagers but not good enough to associate with the gentry. The only visitor we ever had was her particular friend, Mrs. Crimple. I was allowed to attend the dame school until I was twelve because Mrs. Crimple was the instructress, but otherwise we lived alone in our little cottage, and I helped my aunt with her sewing until dark every day. Except Sundays, of course," she added dutifully. "My aunt was very religious. We attended church on Sundays and then returned home and my aunt would read uplifting scriptures to me."

The bleak picture she painted drew pity from the two men, but Allie rejected such offerings. "Unlike Mavis, I was protected and had food on my plate every day. My aunt did her best."

"I'm sure she did," Lord Norwich returned dryly, "but it does not sound like an enjoyable life."

"No . . . no, it was not enjoyable." Allie drew her thoughts from her lonely childhood to return to the story at hand. "When we arrived in London, after several days' travel, my father had the coach stop at a posting inn outside of London and told me to go into the room he had reserved for me and change into the garments he had carried up to it. I discovered a jonquil silk gown, quite beautiful, but unsuited to me. It was several inches too short and did not fit me properly, and the color made me look ill," she explained ruefully, remembering her hopeful approach to the cracked looking glass in the inn's bedroom and her staring horrified at the vision looking back at her. "I looked like a freak."

With a chuckle that surprised her listeners, she added, "And Papa insisted that I wear the matching slippers even though they were too small and pinched my toes quite dreadfully, so that I walked with a mincing gait. I must have been the most shockingly laughable figure! I know your brother . . ." Allie halted abruptly.

"Never fear, Mrs. Montgomery. I am well aware my brother had no gallantry or consideration for others."

"Yes, well, my father then bustled me back into the carriage and we went immediately to the church."

"You went to the church directly upon your arrival in London?" Lord Norwich asked in surprise.

"Yes, my lord. I think Papa was afraid Mr. Montgomery would back out if he saw me before we met at the altar, and I wish to heaven he had," she added quietly.

Lord Norwich studied the woman opposite

him. He pictured her entering the church. No, his brother would not be kind. He must have been desperate to go through with the marriage. But it was the marriage itself, rather than the events leading up to it, that held the greatest interest for him.

Having sunk into a brown study, Allie visibly shook herself before adding, "There is really little else to tell."

Mavis sat silently and Mr. Browning nodded as if her words had confirmed his own opinion, but Lord Norwich reacted quite differently.

"Nothing else to tell? What of your marriage? It lasted one month, did it not?"

"I saw my husband three times after we left the church, my lord," Allie confessed reluctantly.

Astounded, Lord Norwich stared at her, unable to ask the questions whirling around in his head.

Taking pity on him, Allie explained, "Your brother was quite open with me in the carriage after we had left my father and the church behind. He explained that he had married me for the money my father had given him and he had no interest in me. I was to stay out of his way."

"And you did so?" he asked incredulously.

"Yes. I was shocked and upset the first few days and scarcely left my room. But I found the luxury in which I lived an enjoyable change. In about a week, I emerged from my chamber to survey my new home. When Mr. Montgomery was gone, I spent hours in the library poring over the books." Her brown eyes took on a sparkle as she remembered her pleasure. "I had neither the time nor the resources while with my aunt."

"When was the second time you saw Edward?"

"Edward? Oh, uh, I gave in to temptation one day. The weather was beautiful and I longed for a breath of fresh air. I slipped outside just to take a short stroll. I was looking at all the magnificent buildings and interesting people and I stepped into the street without care. I was almost trampled by a curricle. The driver was extremely kind. He pulled up and ascertained my safety. Then he presented his card and offered to escort me home. I told him it was unnecessary since I lived only three doors away. He recognized it as Mr. Montgomery's house and—and asked if I were a relative. I told him I was his wife. He seemed surprised but pleasant. Then I continued my walk, almost forgetting the incident." She paused, swallowing convulsively. "My husband came to my room several days later. I'm still not sure, but I assume he had intended to keep our marriage secret, thereby eliminating any potential scandal when he divorced me." She looked questioningly at Mr. Browning.

"Yes, I believe that was his plan," he concurred.

"Was there no notice sent to the paper?" Lord Norwich questioned. "Surely your father would have demanded that?"

"My father was . . . a social climber, my lord. He was not careful in his negotiations, however. He confused rank with honor."

Her bitter if accurate thrust brought color to the Earl's cheeks.

"I'm sorry, my lord."

"It is of no matter, madam. In the circumstances, you have shown considerable restraint."

When she did not proceed with her explanation, he added, "I assume my brother was less than kind in his interview?"

"He was brutal! I wrote a letter to my father begging him to visit me. But I don't think it was delivered. Once, from the library, I thought I heard his voice, but I got to the hallway too late and the butler denied he was there. I was not allowed to leave the house. I tried to escape one night, thinking the servants would be asleep, but Mr. Montgomery had someone outside my door. I was as much a prisoner then as I was in Newgate. But at least in Newgate I had a friend." She squeezed Mavis's hand gratefully.

Lord Norwich turned to his man of business. "Browning, were you aware of all this?"

"No, my lord. My mother enjoys repeating tidbits of gossip, especially when she knows the person is one of our clients. She informed me one day that it was rumored that Mr. Montgomery would soon marry the Lady Amabel Courtney."

"Did you tell her he was already married?"

"No, my lord. I do not divulge my clients' business to anyone, not even my mother. But naturally I called on Mr. Montgomery, as I was concerned about the situation. He told me his marriage was a secret and a divorce would cause no scandal. I protested that his conduct was dishonorable, but he merely laughed. He warned me not to repeat his intentions to anyone, but I informed him I would no longer handle his affairs. I am sorry, my lord, but I could not continue with such a deception."

"I understand, Browning. How soon after this was he murdered?" Lord Norwich leaned forward on his chair.

"His death occurred the very next evening, my lord," Browning revealed.

"All of the marriage settlement had been transferred to him?" Norwich probed.

"That very day." Browning shook his head, still distressed by the unsettling affair.

Lord Norwich turned back to his sister-in-law. "I assume the night of his death was the last time you saw your husband?"

She nodded, her cheeks flushed, and he couldn't help but notice how charming she appeared in the fire's glow.

"Madam, when you last saw your husband that evening, was he alive or dead?"

She parted her lips to speak, but words failed her.

## Chapter Three

Mavis moved closer to Allie in support. It was not only the question Lord Norwich had asked that alarmed the two women but also his manner. He sounded as if he doubted Allie's innocence. And if that were so, why had he obtained her freedom?

Mrs. Montgomery found her voice and asked Lord Norwich that very question.

"I have only obtained a temporary freedom for you, madam. Now that I have returned to this country, your trial date has been set. A certain personage has allowed you a month to prepare. My man of business, Mr. Browning, is convinced that you are innocent; I am not. But until your trial, I saw no reason for a relative of mine to be housed in Newgate."

Allie wilted before their eyes, her renewed color fading rapidly as she realized her freedom was only temporary. Then some inner strength stiffened her back and she lifted her eyes to look levelly at her brother-in-law. "Thank you for your consideration, my lord. If you will excuse me now, I am rather tired."

As she started to rise, however, Lord Norwich spoke. "As are we all, madam, but you have not yet answered my question. Was my brother alive when you parted from him on that fateful night?"

"Yes, my lord," Allie ground out, "your precious brother was alive, though it was more than he deserved."

"Do you have any proof of that?" He regretted the harshness of his question, but it was imperative that he be informed of the events of that evening.

"If I did, do you not think I would have presented it?"

There was silence after Allie's outburst before Mavis spoke. "She didn't kill him, my lord. She is kind and . . . and good!"

"Perhaps, Mavis," Lord Norwich said softly, "but you must admit she had reason to hate my brother."

"But in prison, even though the others made her life miserable, she never broke. And the little she had she always shared with me."

"I brought as much as I could," Mr. Browning exclaimed in frustration.

"It's all right, Mr. Browning," Allie soothed. "We appreciated what you did so much."

Lord Norwich studied their three faces, seeing there a warm camaraderie from which he was excluded.

"I think perhaps you have misunderstood my questioning, Mrs. Montgomery. I was not trying to convict an innocent person. But I have . . . had no knowledge of my brother's marriage or his wife. I received word from Mr. Browning that he was dead and his wife accused of murder. He added a most eloquent plea for assistance in obtaining her release. I complied with that request. Now, I must determine what transpired that night."

There was a slight relaxation of tension at his words.

"If Mrs. Montgomery is innocent, then we have only one month to find the real culprit, or Mrs. Montgomery will hang for a crime she . . . perhaps did not commit. The crown is satisfied. They have a person with a motive, an opportunity, and a weapon. Why look further? It is up to us to discover the truth."

"A month," Mr. Browning echoed.

"Hang?" Allie whispered.

"Will you help us further, Mr. Browning?"

"I am at your service, my lord. But we do not have much time."

"No, we do not."

"Do you take me for a fool, my lord?" Allie questioned dully as he turned to her. "The murder took place two months ago. How will we be able to prove my innocence?"

"No, I do not take you for a fool. But then I did not take you for a coward, either."

"My lord!"

"Lord Norwich!"

Allie looked up into the dark-haired man's blue eyes, ignoring the others' protests, a small smile stealing onto her face. "I did not think such of myself, my lord, but I find the thought of hanging turns my limbs to water and my mind to jelly."

Lord Norwich pressed her clasped hands before sitting back in his chair.

Allie stared down at her hands, cold and bereft when only a moment ago they had been warm and protected. She forced her eyes up to the Earl's face, dismissing her thoughts. It would be dangerous to place too much faith in the Earl's character. He wanted to salvage what was left of his family's reputation; she wanted to save her life.

"How exactly will you go about finding the real murderer?" she asked, regaining her control.

The Earl had surprised himself too with his announcement of a plan to uncover the real culprit. As yet, he was loath to admit he had no actual ideas of how to go about this. But he was by no means certain now that his sister-in-law was guilty of his brother's murder.

"I think, my dear, that it would be best to end our discussion this evening before we tire you completely. Besides, it will give me a chance to organize my thoughts. Tomorrow, after you have had a good night's rest, we will continue our discussion. If we go over the events of that ill-fated night, I am sure we will find something to tell us where to search."

"Very well, my lord," Allie agreed, rising to her feet. "I do not know how to express my gratitude. If, at times, I have not seemed appreciative of your efforts, I beg you to forgive me."

"There is nothing to forgive. You have been through a difficult time. Sleep well," he added as Jeffers answered his ring. After giving instructions to the butler and watching the two ladies exit the room, the Earl and Mr. Browning looked at each other.

"Sit down, Browning. I will get us something stronger than tea to drink. I think we shall need it." Lord Norwich moved across to where a decanter resided on a silver tray along with several glasses and poured two drinks, returning to where Mr. Browning had resumed his seat.

"Well, man, what do you think?" the Earl asked abruptly just as Mr. Browning was sipping his brandy. "We cannot let that woman hang for the murder of one who didn't deserve to live. I'll not bamboozle you as I did her. To be honest, I have no idea whether we will be able to save her."

In the face of the Earl's earlier calm facade, his

agitated demeanor was even more unsettling. "My lord, surely we can try. It will not be easy, I realize, but what choice do we have?" Browning asked.

"Exactly. Have *you* any ideas, sir?"

With a small, self-conscious cough, Mr. Browning began. "Actually, I have already made some inroads." At the Earl's swift, eager response, he cautioned, "It is just a beginning, my lord. After my efforts on behalf of Mrs. Montgomery had dwindled to the twice-daily visits to Newgate, I decided to study the events of that evening. I had had dealings with your brother's butler on several occasions and knew him to be a rather unsavory character. Because of several facts in my possession, I was able to prompt him on a few items he did not give the Bow Street Runners."

"Such as?"

"Mr. Montgomery was not alone in the house that evening."

"Of course not. His wife and the servants were there. What has that to say to anything?"

"No, my lord. You misunderstand me. Mr. Montgomery did not return home alone that evening. Several of his cronies accompanied him."

"What? Are you sure?"

"Fairly sure, my lord. I could not induce him to name Mr. Montgomery's companions, but he did admit there were two men with him that evening."

"And he did not inform the authorities?"

"No, my lord."

"When was Edward's body discovered?"

"Not until almost noon the next day. He had

dismissed his valet upon his arrival that evening, telling him he would put himself to bed. The butler indicated the men left around two in the morning, several hours after the argument between Mr. and Mrs. Montgomery was overheard by the servants."

"Was Edward seen after their departure?"

"No, my lord. He did not accompany his guests down the stairs." Mr. Browning paused before adding, "That was not thought to be unusual, Lord Norwich."

"No, I realize that." Lord Norwich frowned, staring intently ahead of him. "So there is no proof my brother was alive when his friends left him. All we have to do is discover their names and we have two prime suspects for his murder."

"Suspects, perhaps, my lord. But we do not have proof that Mrs. Montgomery did not murder him. Until we do, I fear the authorities would not listen to us."

"Just the fact that there were two companions should make them reevaluate the situation," Lord Norwich assured the solicitor, relief flooding him. "All we must do is identify those men. Tomorrow, I will go question Brabich . . . it is still Brabich, isn't it?" At Mr. Browning's nod, he continued. "I will question him first thing tomorrow morning. Perhaps I can persuade him to tell me the names of the men."

Mr. Browning opened his mouth to warn Lord Norwich the task might be more difficult than the Earl suspected, but he did not voice his concern. Perhaps the Earl would not take kindly to such intervention. But Mr. Browning, thinking back to

Brabich's white face and shaking hands, awaited the outcome of the Earl's interview with his brother's butler with scant hope of success.

Allie returned to her bed, her head full of jumbled thoughts. She was comforted by Mavis's even breathing, but Allie was unable to follow her lead.

Poor Papa! Tears welled in her eyes as she thought of him. His downfall had been his ambition and his inability to see Mr. Montgomery for the scoundrel he was. But he had paid for it with his life. She could not hate him, in spite of her present difficulties.

At least, thanks to Lord Norwich, she was temporarily spared the wretchedness of prison. Her mind's eye dwelt on the tall, handsome man who had rescued her. His striking appearance would draw female attention anywhere. Allie was sure he was much admired by the ladies of the ton.

When he touched her hands, her heart had fluttered and a melting warmth had stolen over her. But he was Edward's brother, she reminded herself, and could be every bit as cruel. As she snuggled into her down pillow, she found herself wondering just how like his brother he was.

Enough! she warned herself. He was her brother-in-law. He had no interest in her in that way.

She must concentrate on clearing her name and resolving the nightmare in which she found herself. It would not do to waste her time dreaming of a dark-haired man's tender strength, warm hands, brilliant blue eyes. Yet her lips curved in a shy smile even as she drifted off to sleep, and her dreams were filled with visions of Lord Norwich.

Lord Norwich arose at an hour early for a member of the ton. His travels had accustomed him to an early start, and the habit was not an easy one to break. Besides, he was eager to set about clearing the mysteries surrounding his brother's murder.

Arriving at his brother's house on Half Moon Street, he took note of the fact that the knocker had been withdrawn. Undaunted, he used his whip handle to rap smartly upon the door, then tapped it against his highly polished boots impatiently as he awaited a response.

After a second summons, the door swung open slightly and a pale face appeared around the edge of the door. Lord Norwich did not recognize the servant but did not hesitate to make himself known.

"I am Norwich. Open the door, please."

"The master be dead and there be no one 'ere to receive visitors, Mr. Norwich . . . sir," the man hastily added at the caller's frown.

"It is the Earl of Norwich, my good man, and the master was my brother. I have come to talk with Brabich."

The man's eyes widened as his caller identified himself, but the door did not open any farther. "Mr. Brabich not be 'ere right now, me lord. 'Appen 'e'll be 'ere later." The man cleared his throat and straightened his scrawny body, opening the door slightly. "Per'aps I kin be of service, me lord."

Lord Norwich eyed the unprepossessing figure. "Were you employed here the night my brother was killed?"

The eyes became shuttered momentarily before they opened wide. "No, me lord. Mr. Brabich 'ired me after the rest of 'em split."

"I see. Well, you might tell Brabich I will return later this afternoon to discuss my brother's death with him."

"Aye, me lord. I'll tell 'im just that."

Dissatisfied, but having nothing else to say to the man, Lord Norwich turned on his heel and trod down the steps to his curricle, his horses held in check by his groom, Robinson. After he had sprung into his seat, Lord Norwich looked back to see the strange man staring malevolently after him.

Lord Norwich shrugged his shoulders. Perhaps he was becoming fanciful since his return. The man was a stranger. The stare was crude curiosity —nothing more.

In spite of being forestalled of his original purpose, the Earl had a busy morning. He visited Tattersall's to replenish his stables, depleted during his absence. While there, he ran into several old friends and chatted about the happenings in the ton.

He noticed the men carefully avoided any mention of his brother other than to briefly express their condolences. And Lord Norwich did not mention his visit to Newgate. News could fly through the ton at a remarkable rate.

One man's complaining of the modiste's bill he had received from his wife's most recent shopping excursion put Lord Norwich in mind of something else he wanted to do.

"Who is the star in the fashion world this season?" he asked lazily.

Mr. Frobisher, his own attire showing meticulous attention, scornfully said, "My wife says Mme Feydeau is all the crack. But you know women. Next month it will be someone else. All they need is a Frenchy name to draw them in."

"True," Lord Norwich agreed before changing the subject. But after leaving Tattersall's, he instructed Robinson to discover the address of a Mme Feydeau, and soon he was being waited upon in that lady's elegant Bond Street showroom.

Though Mme Feydeau, née Milly Brown, had not previously enjoyed the patronage of the Earl of Norwich, she had made it her business to know all the members of the peerage by reputation and, more exactly, fortune. The Earl of Norwich had no difficulty establishing an account for his sister-in-law, and the couturière was quite willing to travel to the Earl's town house for fittings, accepting his explanation that his sister-in-law was recovering from an extended illness and was not yet able to make shopping expeditions.

Mme Feydeau was a little taken aback when his lordship requested she carry along some dresses for a lady's maid. She almost informed him in her thickest accent that she catered only to the upper crust. However, better judgment overcame her snobbery and she acquiesced calmly.

What did it matter if she dressed a lady's maid as long as the Earl paid the bill. An appointment was made for the following afternoon and the Earl exited the showroom amid the flutterings and whisperings of the ladies gathering there.

The brightness of the sun and a certain emptiness in his stomach reminded the Earl of the passing of time, and he retired to White's, his club, to enjoy a light repast.

He was eagerly greeted by several long-time friends. Though he seldom put in an appearance during the Season, his friends remained true.

The conversation was pleasant throughout the meal, the men bringing out the morsels of gossip that seemed to multiply overnight during the Season. The Earl noted again, however, that the topics of his brother, his secret marriage, and his murder were carefully skirted.

He waited until he and his two particular friends had withdrawn to a quiet book-lined room with large leather chairs where members could isolate themselves from the noise of the dining and gaming rooms.

As he, Lord Caston, and Mr. William Hastings relaxed, the Earl wiped the complacent expressions from his companions' faces. "Now, my friends, why don't you tell me what is being said about my late, unlamented brother."

His friends exchanged guilty looks. Lord Caston assiduously straightened his cravat, ignoring Norwich's stern visage. Mr. Hastings flushed a crimson red.

"D-drat it, Norwich, you shouldn't be surprising me like that. I mean, what's a fellow to think?"

"Cut line, Billy. You and Caston here have been avoiding the subject, but I know it must have made a splash."

"Really, Norwich," Lord Caston drawled, looking down his handsome nose, "you act as if we were the veriest gossips. I protest."

Lord Norwich's lips curved in amusement at those frivolous words, knowing that beneath the pretense was a true friend, no matter what coil a fellow was in.

"I have a need to know, Caston. I'm not looking for idle conversation."

"Then it's true that you've rescued your brother's widow from Newgate?"

"Damn! How did that get around so quickly?"

"Come now, man," Lord Caston protested. "You dare to doubt the underground information system of London? It is more efficient than any army known to mankind."

"Did you really visit that place?" Mr. Hastings asked, his round face sobering intently. "Is it as bad as they say?"

"It is a veritable hellhole. Certainly no place for a gentlewoman."

"Is she?" Lord Caston asked before flushing at his impetuous question. "Sorry, Norwich, I should not have . . . there was much talk. We will be glad to tell you what we know," he quickly offered, still embarrassed at his blatant curiosity.

"Thank you, Caston. I would like to know

when news of my brother's marriage became known."

The two other men exchanged a surprised glance. "Why, not until the woman was arrested. At least, it was rumored that she was his wife. It was several days before it was proved."

"Damn near caused apoplexy among some of the dowagers who think themselves in the know," Billy added with a smirk.

Lord Norwich was too intent on what he had just heard to smile at his friend's amusement. "There was no hint of scandal?"

"Come now, Norwich. You know as well as I that there was always scandal attached to Montgomery's name."

Mr. Hastings nodded in agreement, watching his friend closely.

"What of Lady Amabel Courtney? Was there no talk of a marriage there?" Lord Norwich asked abruptly. Both men's eyes fell to the floor.

"Well." Billy shrugged. "You know how people talk. They are always smelling romance, especially women."

Lord Caston studied his friend's face briefly before addressing himself to Mr. Hastings. "I think we must open our budgets to him, Billy. It is clear he's heard something."

He turned to Norwich. "It's true, Norwich, there was heavy betting that Lady Amabel would have him at last. There had been an attachment for a while, but her parents refused to consider the match because it was common knowledge he was a spendthrift, a gamester, and had already run through the fortune your father left him.

Lord Courtney is ruined, and the possibility of Lady Amabel making an excellent match is limited, it's well known."

"What has she done to incur the wrath of society?"

"Any young woman running with your brother and his cronies would earn the censure of the ton, my friend," Lord Caston explained. "She even visited several of the more unsavory gambling hells with them, sans chaperon."

Lord Norwich frowned. "Was my brother her only suitor?"

"No. But he was her most favored. Scarcely a day passed without their being seen together in the park."

"Who else was in pursuit of Lady Amabel?"

"Several of your brother's cohorts were said to have requested permission to address her, but they were just as ineligible as your brother."

"And how has she reacted to his perfidy?"

"That is the strangest aspect of this entire episode. She has embraced the role of chief mourner, dressing in widow's weeds. At social functions she sits in grieving silence, fanning the flames of gossip. She has also frequently made bitter accusations against, uh, your sister-in-law, and expressed great satisfaction that they intend to hang her."

"Bloodthirsty female. The day your man of business—forgot his name—got the trial stayed until your return, the woman was furious. She raved like a madwoman, crying for blood!" Billy added in distaste.

"She cared about my brother so deeply?"

"I would have said she cared about no one but herself," Lord Caston commented evenly, "though it reflects ill on me as a gentleman to say so."

Lord Norwich stared into space, speculation rife in his mind, while his friends patiently waited. When he rose abruptly from his chair, Mr. Hastings protested, "Here, now! Where are you going? We have scarce heard anything about your travels."

"Sorry, Billy, but that must wait. I have an appointment to keep."

Before he could depart, an idea struck him. "Do you have any idea where Lady Amabel will be this evening?"

"All the ton will be attending the theater this evening," Billy assured him. "Kean makes his debut in *Romeo and Juliet*. Lady Amabel will be in Mrs. Hatchett's party."

"Mrs. Hatchett?"

"Husband's in trade. She's trying to gain entrée to the ton with his money." Billy sniffed.

"Ah. Then I'll be joining you two this evening."

"Of course, Norwich," Caston assured him. "You're always welcome."

Lord Norwich gave a nod and a brief smile, then departed, ignoring their puzzled faces.

Robinson had the curricle waiting and Lord Norwich sprang into his vehicle, inspired with a new vigor. He swung the matched grays out into the center of the street, narrowly missing a ragged urchin, his mind totally absorbed.

Robinson sat patiently behind his employer,

long accustomed to his ways. He had heard all
the tales in the servants' quarters and he knew his
lordship was intent on some aspect of his brother's death, but he'd bet his only topcoat it was
not grief. A nasty piece, that one, and cruel. Why,
the skirts had begun to refuse to work on the
estate, afraid he'd give them a slip on the shoulder whether they was willing or not. Even willing, they always came away with bruises and the
like, and no reward for their troubles.

Both men were aroused from their thoughts by
their arrival at Mr. Montgomery's house on Half
Moon Street. Thrusting the reins into Robinson's
hands, Lord Norwich briskly ascended the steps
and rapped on the door. He stood waiting for a
response, his impatience growing with each moment. Again he knocked, but though he listened
intently, he could detect no sign of a response.

Exasperated, Norwich was poised to pound on
the door a third time when a piercing scream rose
from deep inside the house. He called to Robinson to follow him and pushed against the door.
He was surprised to find it yield easily, and once
inside, he paused only to determine the source of
the scream. He was aided by a rising moan, almost a crooning, from the kitchen area.

Racing down the narrow steps, he halted
abruptly at the sight before him. Kneeling on the
floor was a stout, gray-haired woman cradling the
still form sprawled on the kitchen's stone floor.
Norwich was snapped from his frozen stance by
the clattering descent of his groom, who had de-
layed only to hire a likely-looking lad to watch
the horses before following his master.

"Summon the watch!" he ordered, before gentling his tone to address the woman. "Mrs. Brabich?"

There was no response and Norwich moved closer, laying a gentle hand on her shoulder. "Mrs. Brabich?" The woman looked up but there was no recognition in her dazed eyes. "Mrs. Brabich, it is Lord Norwich. May I be of assistance?"

Her eyes cleared momentarily before they closed and her head sank to lie caressingly against the cold, still face resting on her bosom. "Nay, there's naught to be done. They kilt 'im, you see." There was a sob to accompany the tears streaming down her work-worn face before she repeated in a whisper, "They kilt 'im."

## Chapter Four

When Lord Norwich returned to his residence late that afternoon, his appearance was as elegant as ever. But there was an air of fatigue about him and a certain rigidity in his shoulders that spurred his servants to greater heights in eagerly supplying his needs. Within minutes of his arrival, he found himself ensconced in a large tub of steaming water before a cheerfully crackling fire in his bedroom, the tension generated by his activities gradually easing.

His problems were brought once more to the forefront by the intrusion of his valet, Webster.

"My lord, Mr. Browning has arrived. Jeffers has installed him in the library."

"Thank you, Webster . . . Will Mrs. Montgomery be joining us for dinner?"

"She has requested a tray in her chamber."

"Good. She must rest as much as possible to speed her recovery. I will be attending the theater after dinner, Webster. Perhaps my gray coat?"

Recalled to his duties, Webster laid out the proper attire to maintain his exacting fashion standards for his master, rushing to hold a warm bath sheet for him when he rose from the tub.

When Lord Norwich entered the library, he discovered his guest standing before the fire, enjoying a glass of sherry.

"Browning, forgive my delay."

"Of course, my lord. I arrived but a few minutes ago."

"I have asked Jeffers to begin dinner at once. I have a rendezvous at the theater afterward."

"Of course, Lord Norwich. Uh, has there been a development?"

"Yes."

Motioning for his guest to precede him from the room, Lord Norwich and Mr. Browning entered the dining room.

Mr. Browning had been ruminating about the results of his lordship's discussion with Brabich since receiving his invitation earlier this afternoon. Now his curiosity intensified.

Impassively waiting the withdrawal of his servants, Norwich reviewed his afternoon for the salient points he wished to present to Mr. Browning. He did not have a great deal of time if he was to arrive before the first intermission at the theater.

When the doors closed behind Jeffers, Lord Norwich began his report.

"I learned several interesting facts today. Also, I must tell you that Brabich is no longer with us."

"He has run off? I was afraid that might—"

"He is dead."

"What?"

"He was murdered early this afternoon, thanks in large measure, I am afraid, to my carelessness."

"What happened?"

"I visited my late brother's house this morning. The servant answering the door told me Brabich was not there. He offered his assistance. I thought to question him also, but he assured me he had been hired since my brother's death. When I returned this afternoon, Mrs. Brabich had just discovered her husband dead on the kitchen floor."

"Murdered?"

"A dagger through his heart."

"The same as your brother! Did you notify the Runners?"

"I tried," Lord Norwich replied dryly. "My success was limited."

"I don't suppose the murderer was caught, but did Mrs. Brabich or the other servants know who might have done it?"

"Mrs. Brabich only knew her husband was frightened. He would not tell her why."

"And the other servants?"

"There were no other servants."

"But you said . . ."

"I know. But Mrs. Brabich assured me no additional staff had been hired, and the servants working at the time of my brother's death have found other employment, fearing the house would be closed and sold."

"So who opened the door to you earlier?"

"I don't know. I described him to Mrs. Brabich and she thought she had seen the man talking to her husband once or twice, but when she asked about him, Brabich refused to tell her anything."

"They must have feared Brabich would tell you something," Mr. Browning concluded, a frown marring his smooth forehead. "It is possible Mrs. Brabich is in great danger, Lord Norwich, if they think her husband confided in her."

"Yes, I thought of that. I sent her to her family in York. She pleaded to stay for her husband's burial, but I feared for her safety."

"That is too bad." Mr. Browning paused to partake of his baked salmon. "What is our next step? Have you told Mrs. Montgomery?"

"No. I think Brabich's death would only alarm her, and if she had any knowledge of who accompanied her husband that evening, she would have told us."

"But does the murderer know that?"

Lord Norwich frowned as he considered Mr. Browning's observation. "I am not sure."

"What can I do to assist you?"

"I think it would be helpful if you made discreet inquiries into the financial situation of my brother's cronies, particularly any who might have shown an interest in Lady Amabel Courtney."

"You think jealousy would cause a gentleman to stab a friend?"

"It has been known to happen. And I can think of no other reason. No one will benefit financially from his death except his wife or myself. Perhaps someone owed him a large gambling debt?"

"I will try to discover all that I can. Is there nothing else to be done?"

"I think we should go ahead and settle my brother's will. Sell the town house, his stables, and so forth, if Mrs. Montgomery approves, of course—though I can't think she has any happy memories of it—and store any valuables that she might want at a later date. Transfer all the funds to Mrs. Montgomery. Have you settled her father's estate?"

"No, my lord. His company is functioning under his second-in-command and he has reported to me. I felt Mrs. Montgomery was in no state to make decisions about her father's estate when she was in Newgate. She did not even find out about his death until several days after her incarceration."

"I think you were correct, Browning, but now these things need to be taken care of."

"All right, Lord Norwich. Is there anything else?"

"No, Browning, I think that will be enough to keep you busy for several days. If you discover anything about Edward's friends, let me know."

"And you, my lord? How do you intend to proceed with your investigation?"

"I, my dear Browning, shall become acquainted with one Lady Amabel Courtney. I am not sure how she is connected with the events other than the obvious, but something strikes me very strangely about her actions."

"In what way?"

"She is wearing widow's weeds. I am anxious to discover just how deep a relationship she actually had with my brother."

Though his evening was to be spent in pursuit of Lady Amabel, Lord Norwich's thoughts were still on the young woman abovestairs. Her fragile courage, her gentle strength, her large eyes, those images had fortified his determination to clear his sister-in-law of murder.

On impulse, he stopped by her room before his departure for the theater. He wanted to assure himself she had everything she needed. When there was no answer to his soft knock, he hesitated and then opened the door. It was dark in the room except for a shaft of early moonlight streaming through the window. The only noise was the rhythmic breathing of the two sleeping women. He should leave at once, he knew, but something drew him to the big bed. Pulling back the bed curtains, he stood staring down at the young woman newly come into his life.

Her brown hair was plaited down her back, her dark lashes shadowing her hollow cheeks. Involuntarily, he reached out to caress that cheek. When she turned her face into his hand, Lord Norwich was surprised at the rush of desire that flooded him. She was pretty, even thin as she was, and something about her gentle nature clutched at his heart.

Stepping back from temptation, he left the room. She was a member of his family and under his protection. She was also, he reminded himself, an accused murderess, and although he thought the world was well rid of Edward, he had an obligation to see that his killer was brought to justice.

An elegantly dressed Lord Norwich, his dark hair styled à la Brutus, slipped into Lord Caston's box moments before the first intermission. Only his friend, however, noted his belated arrival since, for once, all attention was riveted upon the stage. Though he sent him a quizzical glance, no words were spoken.

When the curtain fell on the first act and the ton resumed its gossiping, flirting, seeing, and being seen, it took only a moment for Lord Norwich to locate his quarry. Seated in a box directly opposite was a handsome young woman dressed totally in black from the feathers in her cascading golden curls to the tips of her satin slippers.

It was a startling ensemble among the debutantes' pastels and the bright plumage of the matrons. As a ploy to gain attention in the ever more elegant ton, it was clever, Lord Norwich admitted. He wondered cynically, however, if the young woman would have dressed so had the color not emphasized her golden hair or her perfect peaches and cream complexion.

Leaning close to Lord Caston, he asked, "I assume the lady in black is Lady Amabel?"

"Can you doubt it? She seems determined to be a constant reminder of your brother's death."

"Which is strange, since he betrayed her," Lord Norwich muttered, his eyes never leaving the figure of mourning. As a florid gentleman in a yellow waistcoat moved over to the stunning Beauty, he asked, "Who is that?"

Lord Caston glanced carelessly in the lady's direction before turning back to his friend. "One of your brother's ne'er-do-well friends, Sir Harold Baynham. He has been, uh, in attendance upon Lady Amabel since Montgomery's death."

"Ah yes. I believe Edward introduced me last year when I was in town briefly. I shall go renew our acquaintance."

Ignoring his friend's startled expression, Lord Norwich exited the box, his broad shoulders moving easily through the ever-growing crowd seeking refreshment or the latest *on dit* until he reached the entrance of the box. Entering, he found himself, after his audience had recovered from their surprise, warmly greeted. When Sir Harold in his turn acknowledged the newcomer with a trace of apprehension, Lord Norwich launched his campaign.

"Sir Harold, I am delighted to have this opportunity to greet you. As one of my brother's friends, I realize this has not been an easy time for you."

"Uh, no, my lord. Nor for you either," the man added hastily.

"No," Lord Norwich concurred in a slightly mournful manner, "it has not. It was a sad return to my mother land." He paused, glancing at his audience, afraid he might have overplayed his sorrow, but he saw only sympathy from all but Sir Harold. There a certain wariness was visible. "But I must not burden you with my problems. I purposely came, Sir Harold, to ask a favor of you." He paused again, enjoying the panic spreading across the man's face. "Would you be so kind as to introduce me to the Lady Amabel Courtney? I feel my brother betrayed her mightily and I would like to offer my apologies."

"O'course, my lord, o'course," the man responded with relief, turning at once to the Beauty in black. "Belle, here's Lord Norwich, Montgomery's brother, you know."

Norwich moved forward, observing his target curiously. Her only flaws were a certain coldness of manner and pettishness about the mouth. But Lord Norwich's eligibility earned him a brilliant smile and a throaty greeting.

"Lord Norwich! It is a pleasure to meet Edward's brother." The pouting lips and fluttering lashes were intended to captivate and Lord Norwich obliged, bending low over her hand, his lips resting briefly on her black glove.

"Lady Amabel, I feel I have much to apologize for. May I call upon you tomorrow . . . in private?"

Lord Norwich noted both a jealous stiffening in Sir Harold and excited calculation on Lady Amabel's part. The Earl of Norwich would be a larger prize in the marriage mart than Lady Amabel had hoped for. She assented with a breathless, "Of course, my lord."

With another reverent kiss to the hand he had

continued to hold, Lord Norwich rose to depart but found Sir Harold blocking his passage.

"My lord," he began truculently, "I have heard that you are sheltering your brother's murderer!"

Lord Norwich observed his accoster coolly before replying simply, "I obtained the temporary release of my sister-in-law from Newgate prison."

"Are you not afraid she might kill you next?" the man sneered.

"No, Sir Harold, I have no fear of that."

"That was your brother's mistake."

"Was it, Sir Harold? Are you so very sure of that?" Though his words were spoken softly, silence had fallen in the box at the beginning of their confrontation and no one missed the final exchange. Without waiting for an answer, Lord Norwich excused himself. Out in the hall, however, his control was not as absolute.

"Damn," he muttered softly. He had intended to play his cards more cautiously. He did not want to make an issue of Mrs. Montgomery's innocence with either Sir Harold or Lady Amabel. Perhaps he could allay any suspicions Lady Amabel might have when he called on her on the morrow.

Lady Amabel's behavior was a puzzle to him, though. As he strolled back to Lord Caston's box, absentmindedly greeting friends and acquaintances in the crowd, he wondered why she continued to advertise her humiliation. She did not appear to be the type to suffer slights gladly. Either she truly loved his brother or . . . or she was privy to his plans. If that were true, then

Billy was right. A more bloodthirsty female did not exist. How could a woman accept, nay, encourage, such cruelty to another woman, and then demand her head when, if, she sought relief.

Lord Norwich realized he no longer cared whether or not Mrs. Montgomery had murdered her husband. She was clearly the victim and he was determined she would suffer no more for his brother's sins. Though he returned to Lord Caston's box for the rest of the evening, his mind dwelt on the gentle, courageous figure whose very being had dominated his life since his return to England.

Allie stretched drowsily in the luxurious bed, unconsciously enjoying the comfort she had seldom experienced in her life. Opening her eyes one at a time, she surveyed her surroundings in the early morning light, delighting in the pale yellow silk bed hangings, the cream walls, the matching yellow drapery through which the increasingly bright light was filtered.

It was not for several minutes that she noticed her well-being. After only two days she had difficulty recalling the real agony of the past two months. Her face clouded when she remembered her brother-in-law's warning that this freedom was only temporary.

She hunched her shoulders under the bedclothes and buried her nose in her pillow as if that fact would disappear if she refused to face the day. Several minutes of such ruminations, however, was enough and she sat up in bed, prepared to determine her course of action.

She had not seen Norwich at all the preceding day. She had slept most of the day, rising only for a couple of hours in the evening to partake of another delicious meal. Now that her body was recovering, she felt more optimistic about her future. Perhaps Lord Norwich had devised a plan to save her. It was easy to place her confidence in him. He was tall, strong, with considerate manners and a warm smile, the kind of fairy-tale prince who always rescued the fair maiden. And he had already rescued her from prison.

How ironic that one brother was the cause of her imprisonment while the other had brought about her release. Ironic, too, that society had considered Mr. Montgomery to be the more handsome of the two. Mr. Montgomery's behavior had wiped out any early admiration Allie had had for his blond good looks. Lord Norwich, though without the classic beauty of his half-brother, was a commanding figure, with virile strength, whose smile brightened an otherwise stern face. The black, bristling brows were scarcely noticeable when his blue eyes twinkled.

Eager to talk to her brother-in-law again, Allie threw back the bedclothes and slipped quietly from her bed. Mavis was sleeping soundly on the narrow trundle bed hastily prepared for her.

Allie was as concerned about her new abigail as she was herself. If she were hanged, what would become of Mavis? In addition to the very real debt she owed the girl, she wanted a better life for her. If she were free, her inheritance from her father alone would be sufficient to care for both of them the rest of their lives.

Perhaps she and Mavis would purchase a cottage in the Lake District. She had always wanted to visit that area of England, but the thought of leaving her brother-in-law's home made her uneasy. She banished the image of Lord Norwich from her mind. He had nothing to do with her future, she reminded herself. She must not long for . . . count on his presence in her future.

And if the unthinkable happened, could she trust Lord Norwich to look after Mavis? Yes, she answered herself with deep conviction, he was an honorable man. If he agreed to her plans, he would follow through. And there was always Mr. Browning.

She would ask him about her father's estate, the mills up north, his investments. And, if she was allowed to make purchases, she would pay for new gowns for herself and Mavis. Not serviceable gray, either, but something soft and pretty. If she were not to be much longer for this world, she was filled with a great determination to enjoy what few days remained to her. And she would like Lord Norwich to see her in elegant finery, she admitted, instead of her mournful gray.

Dressing speedily, without the services of Mavis, Allie slipped into her most presentable morning gown, gray, of course, rebraided her brown hair, winding the long plait around the top of her head in a coronet, and proceeded down the stairs.

Though she was sure Lord Norwich would not be up, having learned during the few weeks of her marriage that noon was considered the top of the morning by the ton, Allie hoped to find Jeffers or a footman who could direct her to the dining room and ensure her receiving an early breakfast. Therefore, it was with considerable surprise, and pleasure, that she discovered the dining room already occupied by her brother-in-law.

"My lord! I hope I am not intruding. I did not think you would be up and about yet."

"Of course you are not intruding, madam," Norwich hastily assured her, rising to his feet and motioning for her to join him at a small table set in a bay window overlooking the rear garden. His eyes ran over her figure, noting the improvements in her appearance. Her color had been restored and her brown eyes gleamed.

"How charming," Allie exclaimed, as a footman assisted her into the chair opposite his lordship.

"Yes, it is my favorite view from the entire house. Of course, that might be influenced by Cook's excellent breakfasts always enjoyed at this table."

"I can see where that might sway your opinion, my lord," Allie agreed, a smile on her lips, "but as I have not yet partaken of your cook's breakfasts and yet have confirmed your opinion, I think we may safely allow the view to be passable."

"Delightful. I make you my compliments," Lord Norwich said, smiling lazily as he gazed at her before instructing Jeffers to bring breakfast for his companion. "Are you feeling quite the thing, madam?"

"Yes, thank you, my lord. I am amazed at how swiftly I have recovered. Thank you for—Is something wrong, my lord?" Allie asked, disturbed by the drawing together of Lord Norwich's dark brows.

"Not precisely wrong. It is simply that such formality is unnecessary between family members. It we continue to address each other so, we will have to give up conversation altogether."

"Surely not, my lord," Allie teased, a smile on her lips once more.

"My name is John, and I would that you use it."

"Please, if we are to be informal, John, call me Allie. It is short for Allison."

"I will be delighted to call you Allie, my dear," Lord Norwich assured her, surprising her by reaching across the small table and lifting her hand to his lips, smiling into her luminous brown eyes.

It was only when Jeffers entered with a fresh pot of tea that they became conscious of the fact that Mrs. Montgomery's hand was still resting in Lord Norwich's. Her cheeks growing even more rosy, Allie snatched back her hand and rested it in her lap, her eyes refusing to meet those either of her handsome companion or the elderly butler.

"Allie, do you care for kippers, eggs, toast?"

With a self-conscious laugh, she responded, "All of it, my lord . . . John. I cannot seem to get enough of Cook's delicious food."

Silence reigned while the butler attended to Allie's needs. While waiting for her breakfast, Allie recalled the most important thing she had to discuss with Lord Norwich. His unexpected presence had put the question of her future completely from her mind.

"John, have you determined a plan . . . for proving my innocence?" she asked as soon as Jeffers had departed.

"We are working on several things, Allie. It is looking very promising."

When it appeared he would add nothing more, giving his attention to the breakfast before him, Allie prompted, "Is there anything I can do? Can you tell me what you have discovered?"

Lord Norwich looked up into her anxious brown eyes and his resolve to keep his sister-in-law removed from their efforts began to disintegrate. But he made one last effort. "You must not worry about it, Allie. Mr. Browning and I will not rest until we have rescued you."

"And I am just supposed to sit in the drawing room doing needlework, I suppose?" His bewildered expression did not ease her frustration. "Lord Norwich, I have much to be grateful to you for, but I did what I was told when I agreed to marry your brother, and look what it has brought me. I refuse to be treated as a doll to sit upon a shelf."

"A lady does not . . . a lady cannot involve herself in such a—a tawdry situation."

In exasperation, Allie protested, "I am already involved. *I* am the one they will hang if the real murderer is not found!"

"I realize that, Mrs. Montgomery," Lord Norwich responded stiffly, their earlier understanding complete forgotten, "and I have promised to do my best. Do you doubt my word?"

Allie drew a deep breath and leaned back in her chair, choosing her words with care. She already knew her brother-in-law well enough to recognize the danger signs. "My lord, I do not doubt you, either your word or your ability, but . . . but my life is hanging in the balance. I would know what is happening. I would discover what I might do to assist you. As you said, we only have a month. Surely, even you cannot afford to reject assistance when it is offered."

Lord Norwich shoved his chair back from the table and sprang to his feet to pace back and forth beside the table.

"Madam, I am only trying to protect you. It is my duty as your husband's brother to do so. This could be dangerous and . . . and ugly."

"Do you not think it was ugly and dangerous in Newgate, my lord? Do you not think hanging will be ugly . . . and extremely dangerous?" Allie took pity on his confusion and rose from the table to go to him. She placed a trembling hand on his arm. "My lord . . . John . . . I know that ladies do not enter into a man's business, his activities, but this is *my* business, *my* life. And if I only have one month of my life left, I refuse to sit doing needlework, excluded from the attempts being made to save it."

Lord Norwich took her small hand in both of his and carried it to his lips before saying, "But I do not know of anything you can do, Allie. I am feeling my way. I am ashamed to admit it, but I have no plan of action. I am grasping at straws."

"You could at least tell me what you have discovered, what straws you have grasped. Could you not do that?" she pleaded, her face lifted to his, piercing his reservations.

"Yes . . . yes, I can do that, but you may not enjoy what I am about to tell you, Allie. It is not a pretty tale." He led her back to the table to resume their seats, reluctantly releasing her hand as he moved to his own chair.

Allie sat patiently while John explained his and Mr. Browning's theory that the men accompanying her husband home that evening had remained there until after their argument and then murdered her husband and slipped away.

She was unable to stifle a gasp when he told of discovering Brabich's body and spiriting away Mrs. Brabich to safety, but she said nothing. Her eyes sharpened when he told of Lady Amabel's public behavior and her demand that Allie hang. It was his plan to call on Lady Amabel, "to apologize for my brother's dastardly behavior," that roused Allie to object.

"You are going to call on that woman?" she demanded, her cheeks flushed.

"Yes, I must. At best, my brother betrayed her by marrying you. But I suspect her ladyship was part of his plan. She may perhaps be able to give me some information."

"You are going to tell her of our . . . our search for clues?"

"Not precisely. But her reaction to the news of your release will be interesting."

Allie sat thinking before asking bluntly, "Is she pretty?"

"Why do you ask such a question?"

"She wishes me dead. Perhaps she will charm you into agreeing with her," Allie explained, though she knew it was not the whole truth.

"She will be able to do nothing of the sort. And, yes, she is a Beauty, but . . . there is something about her that I cannot like."

"When do you go to call on her? Perhaps I could come."

"No, of course you could not come."

"But . . ."

"Besides, you will be busy with Mme Feydeau this morning."

"Mme Feydeau? What do you mean?" Allie asked distractedly.

"I made arrangements with Mme Feydeau, the couturière, to come fit you for something more suitable than that gray thing you are wearing."

"Oh! How wonderful! Thank you, John! I meant to ask Mr. Browning if I had received my inheritance from my father so that I could provide some new things for us. May we have the bills sent to Mr. Browning?"

"Of course."

"But I do not yet know if my father's will has been settled. What if . . ."

"The bill will be paid, Allie."

"But . . ."

"Allie!" John roared. "Ladies do not bother their heads about bills and such. Just order what pleases you and Mr. Browning will pay the bill."

"Yes, John," Allie agreed meekly, planning all the while to write a note to Mr. Browning as soon as Lord Norwich left the house.

"And no nip-farthing order. If you want to help, you must be able to go about in society without drawing undue attention to yourself."

"But if . . . if I only have a month . . ."

"Don't argue with me, madam! I expect to see you suitably clothed as soon as Mme Feydeau can manage it."

"Yes, John," she said demurely, her lashes fluttering to her cheeks to hide the excitement there. As he started to leave the room, she hastily added, "And you will tell me what transpires between you and Lady Amabel?"

"If you keep your end of the bargain and order some pretty gowns, perhaps a pink one to match your cheeks, I will tell you what information I gain from Lady Amabel."

The door closed behind him and Allie resumed her breakfast, a smile on her face as she thought about the new clothes she would soon acquire, such thoughts pushing the darker ones away, at least for the moment.

When Mr. Browning arrived in response to Mrs. Montgomery's note, he entered the library, his eyes rapidly searching. But only Mrs. Montgomery awaited him.

"Good morning, Mr. Browning. Thank you for coming so soon."

"I am always at your service, Mrs. Montgomery."

"I wanted to see you because Lord Norwich has summoned a dressmaker on my behalf and I wanted to be sure . . ."

When their business was completed, Mr. Browning hesitated, then said, "Mrs. Montgomery, may I see Mavis for a moment? If you remember, I collected her personal things from her employer and I've been holding them for her. I brought them with me today."

"Of course, Mr. Browning. I'm sure Mavis will be very grateful." She moved to the bellpull and instructed the butler to summon Mavis and also a tea tray.

When Mavis entered the library, she found Allie and Mr. Browning calmly sharing tea. Her eyes eagerly traced Mr. Browning's handsome features before she demurely took a seat by Allie.

Allie looked at the shy girl beside her and then at the distinguished blond man across from her. With a secret smile, she rose to her feet, immediately followed by the other two.

"I must have a word with Jeffers. Shall I have him send in the . . . the package, Mr. Browning?"

"Yes, please."

When Mrs. Montgomery left the room, Mavis swung around to look questioningly at Mr. Browning.

He stepped forward to take her hands in his, surveying her shining gold hair, her blue eyes framed by golden lashes, and swallowed a lump in his throat. "When Mrs. Montgomery asked me to free you from the prison, I . . ."

There was a rap on the door and a footman entered carrying a cheap carpetbag that Mavis immediately recognized. "My bag!" She turned painfully eager eyes to Browning. "Is it my things? Oh, Mr. Browning, did you get my things for me?"

"Yes, Miss Thompson, I did. Your, uh, employer was reluctant to let me have them, but I think I got everything."

Before he finished, Mavis had withdrawn her fingers and rushed to the bag the footman had deposited on the carpet. Browning dismissed him and watched as the young woman opened the bag. She drew out a locket on a slender chain and stared at it in disbelief as tears streamed down her face.

"Miss Thompson, don't cry!" Mr. Browning urged as he put his hands on her shoulders to lift her from the floor. "I thought it would please you."

Gulping, Mavis turned back to the tall gentleman who had become very important to her. "It has, Mr. Browning. I'm very happy. You see, this was my mother's. It is the only thing I had left that was hers. I never thought I'd see it again." With a rush of tears, she cast herself into his arms.

Mr. Browning had no hesitation in wrapping his arms around the damp bundle of femininity. But when Mavis realized what she had done, she pulled away from him, embarrassed.

"Thank you so much. I'm sorry I forgot myself. I . . . you've been so good to me. If I can ever . . . I will do anything for you, Mr. Browning. Thank you, thank . . ." With a hurried curtsy, she thanked him all the way to the door, picking up her bag on the way. And then she was gone, closing the door behind her.

Mr. Browning stood still in the center of the library, reliving the past few minutes with a bemused smile.

# Chapter Five

When Mme Feydeau arrived, she was immediately taken to Mrs. Montgomery's sitting room and led inside by a blond girl in an ugly gray gown.

"Come in, Mme Feydeau," Mavis said quietly. "Please be seated. Mrs. Montgomery will be with you in a moment."

The elegantly attired dressmaker, a believer in advertising her own wares, did as requested, her back ramrod straight. "Are you the abigail for whom I was requested to supply gowns?"

"Yes, madam."

"Just recently hired, I suppose. Well, we can do much better than what you are wearing, but, of course, it must be gray."

"Must it?" Allie asked as she entered her sitting room. "I find that color so depressing."

Mme Feydeau rose and curtsied to her customer. "Good day, Mrs. Montgomery," she said respectfully before adding, "It is what the other abigails are wearing."

Mavis pressed a finger to Allie's arm and she nodded reluctantly. "Of course, I do not want to call undue attention to my—my servant."

"I have several acceptable styles for a servant's gown that will be more attractive than that thing she is wearing," Mme Feydeau said scornfully.

"Good, let me see what you have."

For the next two hours, the women discussed styles, chose fabrics brought in by the dressmaker's minions waiting in the hall, and took measurements. Allie was mesmerized by the richness and color of the many fabrics. Never had she owned so many gowns in her life, but she had no intention of allowing Lord Norwich to complain about her wardrobe. And it would be so glorious, she thought as she wrapped her arms around herself, to appear before him in one of Mme Feydeau's elegant concoctions.

"May I have the pink gown made up first?" she requested with a blush.

"Certainly, madame," the woman agreed. "A wise choice. It will look splendid on your elegant figure. I believe I shall be able to send it and, perhaps, the lilac gown by tomorrow afternoon, along with some undergarments. And I have several suitable dresses already made up that can be fitted to your abigail."

"That quickly? Oh, that is marvelous, madame!"

When the woman had withdrawn, along with her assistants, Allie jumped to her feet to swing Mavis around the room. "Is it not wonderful, Mavis?"

"Yes, it is. You will look beautiful," Mavis assured her with a warm smile.

"I wish you did not have to continue to wear gray."

"It is of no matter. And the white trim you added made my gown much more elegant."

"I suppose. One day, Mavis, when we have resolved our difficulties, you shall have pretty gowns, too."

Mavis moved about the room, restoring order, only nodding in response. She had learned not to count on tomorrow.

Allie wandered back into her bedroom, her mind on the new gowns. For the first time in her life, she would be beautifully dressed. Perhaps Lord Norwich would notice the improvement. Perhaps he would even . . . No! She must concentrate on her problems, not on pipe dreams concerning a certain handsome man.

Lord Norwich had hoped to find Lady Amabel Courtney alone when he called on her to offer his apologies, and he was almost granted his wish. Though respectable young ladies never received without a chaperon, his friends' comments and the warm encouragement he had received from the lady the previous evening had led him to believe she would be alone.

The butler showed him into the drawing room, where Lady Amabel reclined on an Egyptian daybed, the bodice of her black morning gown cut so low he feared for her modesty if she moved. When his eyes were able to leave off his assessment of her attire, he discovered the rigid back of

Sir Harold, who was staring out the window, his bottle-green coat melting into the draperies.

Bending low over his hostess's hand, Lord Norwich said, "Good morning, Lady Amabel . . . and Sir Harold. Thank you so much, my dear lady, for receiving me. I would not have blamed you if you had cut me dead after my brother's reprehensible behavior."

"It is of no matter," Lady Amabel assured him, her long lashes fluttering as she gazed sweetly up at him. "I loved your brother. It is not his fault that woman stabbed him."

That was certainly taking the battle into his camp, Norwich thought. He answered carefully as he sat down beside his hostess. "Murder, of course, cannot be tolerated, but surely, even loving him as you did, you feel some anger that he courted you under false pretenses."

The look of wide-eyed innocence disappeared and one of sophistication took its place. "Really, my lord, surely you knew that Edward undertook the marriage with my knowledge and that it would not prevent our being wed."

"But do you not feel some sympathy for Mrs. Montgomery, to be cheated so?"

Lady Amabel's blue eyes hardened. "She's a merchant's daughter, my lord. She should have remained with her own kind."

Perhaps Lord Norwich's face revealed a semblance of his revulsion, because Lady Amabel immediately softened her expression. "Of course, I wished the poor thing no harm, until she murdered dear Edward. But I believe she should be punished for such a vile deed!"

"I, too, feel that justice should be done, my lady, but I am not sure Mrs. Montgomery is guilty."

"What?" Sir Harold asked sharply, revealing his attentiveness to their conversation.

"I am not sure she has the strength or temperament for such an act."

"You have a tendre for a merchant's daughter?" Lady Amabel demanded.

"No, of course not, dear lady," he lied swiftly. "She is a drab little thing, particularly when compared to you, my lady." Lady Amabel preened before his eyes. "But I feel some responsibility. After all, she is my sister-in-law."

"You can dismiss those ridiculous sentiments, my lord. Edward certainly did not consider her his wife, and if she had not murdered him, I would now be Mrs. Montgomery, not that vulgar nothing!"

"And that is the very reason I am here," Lord Norwich inserted smoothly. "I feel a responsibility to you, as my brother's, uh, intended. May I assist you in any way? I would be glad to provide escort for you. Perhaps you would care for a ride in the park? It is lovely weather outside, though not so lovely as you."

Lady Amabel returned to the role of blushing debutante, though with a speculative gleam in her eye. "I would love a ride in the park this morning, my lord. Several of the old tabbies have snubbed me because I wear mourning for my beloved Edward. It will be good for them to see that we are united in our grief."

"Of course, Lady Amabel. But I can't help

thinking that Edward, who so much admired your beauty, as do I, would have hated seeing you in unrelieved black."

"You do not think I look charming, my lord?" Lady Amabel pouted, leaning forward, further exposing her bosom to his view.

Taking one of her small hands in his, Lord Norwich raised it to his lips before murmuring, "You must always appear charming, no matter what your dress, dear Lady Amabel."

She pressed closer to him, purring, "You must call me Belle, and I will call you John, since we were almost family."

"Belle!" Sir Harold interrupted, appearing agitated. "You promised you would accompany me to Hyde Park."

"But surely, Harry, you will not mind relinquishing your prior claim to Lord Norwich. After all, *it is important* to Lord Norwich to show his concern for my suffering."

It was clear to Norwich that Sir Harold was being brought to heel by his hostess, and he was not surprised to hear him acquiesce to Lady Amabel.

"I would invite you to join us, Sir Harold, but my curricle will hold only Lady Amabel and myself."

"I will just go fetch a bonnet and wrap, John. I will only to be a moment," Lady Amabel said, her eyes promising even more as she brushed against the now standing Lord Norwich before leaving the room.

An awkward silence followed her departure, broken by Sir Harold's gruff voice. "I feel it only fair to warn you that Belle and I are to be married."

Lord Norwich looked at him in surprise. "I was not aware of that, Sir Harold. You are to be congratulated. It must have appeared in the papers before my return to England."

The other man squirmed under the Earl's inquisitive regard. "It ain't been in the papers yet. Her parents . . . asked that we wait until talk of your brother's death has died down."

"Ah yes. I should think you would hasten that day could you but discourage Lady Amabel from wearing black."

"Belle goes her own road. Besides, it's your fault. If it weren't for that interfering man of yours, that woman would have already hanged— and then Belle could give up this nonsensical mourning."

Lord Norwich watched Sir Harold pace the room as they talked, picking up objects and immediately setting them down. "That explains your eagerness to hang an innocent woman, certainly."

"Innocent? Who says she's innocent?" Sir Harold bellowed. Under Lord Norwich's cool stare, he swallowed convulsively. "The authorities say she's guilty."

"Yes, I know, but . . . some additional evidence has come to light."

"Additional evidence? What're you . . ."

Lady Amabel reentered the drawing room, a self-satisfied smile on her face. Before she could extend her hand to Lord Norwich, however, Sir Harold rushed forward.

"Belle! Norwich here thinks someone else killed Edward!"

"Nonsense, Harry! Get hold of yourself. No one else could have killed him but Mrs. Montgomery." Her words were spoken firmly and with an undercurrent of warning.

Norwich watched the two of them speculatively. Lady Amabel, catching his regard, resumed the role of the debutante, fluttering her lashes and placing a soft white hand on the sleeve of his blue superfine coat.

"Shall we go, my lord? I have heard it said you are a famous whip, and I am looking forward to riding with you."

"Of course, Belle. Good day, Sir Harold."

Leading her from the room, Lord Norwich escorted her down the stairs and out to the street where Robinson had the curricle waiting. After handing the lady up into the curricle, he dismissed his groom and joined her. Little conversation was exchanged until their arrival at Hyde Park, but there Lord Norwich was able to give his attention to his companion.

She was already receiving a great deal of attention from the bucks as they ogled her revealing gown. The ladies were attempting to ignore her presence, though it was difficult to do while their escorts could not tear their eyes away. Lord Norwich hoped they could manage the drive without incident and that he would see no one for whose opinion he really cared.

"I understand from Sir Harold that you are to be married soon." The Earl watched as surprise and then consternation crossed her features before Lady Amabel smiled up at him.

"I am afraid Harry is jumping the gun. My parents have refused him permission. And, truly, Harry and I are friends, but . . . I seek something more in a husband." The play of her lashes and demure ducking of her head would have been perfect if she could only have called up a blush at will, but Lord Norwich suspected little remained on earth that could embarrass Lady Amabel.

"I am glad to hear it, Belle. I would hate to have the ton's leading Beauty already spoken for, just when I am considering entering the wedded state. After all, now that my brother is gone, I must think of the succession."

"Of course, my lord," Belle concurred breathlessly, pressing against his arm.

"While you are in mourning, none of us aspiring bucks would dare to intrude, of course." He paused in his conversation to bow a greeting to a well-fed dowager in puce satin accompanied by a charming young woman in a soft blue ruffled and beribboned gown, her gold curls framing her face. "But I am not in a great hurry. It has been some time since I have stayed in London for the Season."

With concealed amusement, he watched his companion struggle with her dilemma, wondering if she was greedy enough to dump Sir Harold and her "mourning" to make herself available for his supposed search for a wife.

Lady Amabel interrupted his musing. "I grieve over your brother's death, my lord, of course, but

I wear mourning to remind the ton that justice has not yet been done." Her carefully demure expression hardened slightly. "And they will not be able to hold off justice much longer." When Norwich made no response, she continued. "I have heard the trial is set for the end of the month. When she has been punished, I will leave off wearing mourning."

Lord Norwich sighed under his breath. His ploy to alter Lady Amabel's behavior had failed . . . and yet she would still consider him husband material. And if her pursuit were no more subtle than her gown, life could become highly embarrassing, not to say difficult, for the next few weeks.

Lord Norwich discovered just how difficult things had become when he arrived home. Jeffers, with a relieved sigh, hastened to explain.

"My Lord, Lady Norwich has arrived! She is demanding to know the location of Mrs. Montgomery."

"Have you told her she is here?" the Earl demanded.

"No, my lord, but . . . but Lady Norwich is very . . . very unsettled."

"Yes, I'm sure she is," Lord Norwich drawled, memories of previous scenes with his stepmother leaving him in no doubt of her hysteria. "Where is . . ."

"John," Allie called, descending the stairs, a bright smile on her face. "Mme Feydeau is wonderful! I cannot thank you enough for . . ."

"Aha!" The drawing room door was thrown

open and a tall, Junoesque woman, her hair an improbable shade of gold and her over-rouged cheeks a bright red, pointed a finger at the now apprehensive Mrs. Montgomery.

"You are the Circe who betrayed my son and struck him down in his prime! How dare you show your face here!"

"She dares because I invited her." The icy tones of her stepson reminded the older woman of his presence.

Whirling to face him, she spit out, "I heard that you had betrayed your brother's memory, but I could not—would not believe you could do such a thing until I saw it with my own eyes!"

The venom spewing from his stepmother was loud enough to draw the servants. No one ever shouted in Lord Norwich's home. Catching sight of Mavis peering down from the second-floor landing, Lord Norwich commanded, "Mavis, come assist Mrs. Montgomery to her room. I believe she should lie down for a time."

Fortunately, he was moving toward Allie as he spoke, for with the realization that her target was to be put beyond her reach, Lady Norwich let forth a screech of rage and charged the younger woman.

Intercepting the attacker just before she reached Allie, the Earl held her fast while Mavis assisted a white and shaken Allie to her room. Once she was out of sight, Lord Norwich released his stepmother, but he kept himself between her and the stairway.

"Madam! Control yourself! You bring dishonor to our name."

"I? I bring dishonor? How can you say so? I only seek justice! How can you be so unfeeling as to harbor that murderess under your roof!"

Lord Norwich's anger dissipated somewhat as he saw the tears gather in her eyes and recognized her very real grief. Whatever his brother had been, this woman had loved him.

"Madam, I understand your grief, but you are in error. Mrs. Montgomery did not kill Edward. I am convinced of that."

"Oh! I see! She has charmed you just as she did my son! Well, you had better be on your guard or they will find you with a dagger in your heart, too!"

"Your son committed a grievous wrong against his wife. Would you allow me to explain the situation to you?"

"Now that he is no longer here to defend his name, you would blacken it for him? You always resented him! Always! You never gave him the consideration due him! But your father loved him best! That you cannot change!"

The Earl winced at her statement but retained a tight hold on his temper. "I admit Edward and I were . . . were never close. But I am a fair man."

"Fair? Hah! If you will not do something about that . . . that . . . woman, I will!"

"No! It was Edward who made her a member of our family and as such I owe her my protection. If you cannot reconcile yourself to that, you must leave."

"You would bar me from my own house?" Lady Norwich demanded incredulously.

"You were mistress here during my father's

lifetime, but it is my house now. You are welcome here as my guest."

"Very well. I will leave *your* house. But do not expect me to ever forget this betrayal. And be warned," she added in dire tones, "I will ensure that that woman pays for the murder of my son."

Norwich turned to find a pale-faced Jeffers standing at his elbow. "Shall I call a hackney for her ladyship, my lord?"

"Yes, please, Jeffers, she is leaving now."

The burning eyes Lady Norwich flashed at him were those of an unbalanced person, and their memory stayed with him even after the door had closed behind her and calm had returned to his house.

"Jeffers, I think we are going to have to protect Mrs. Montgomery from those who would do her harm. Any package that arrives for Mrs. Montgomery must be brought to me for my inspection. And I will interview any callers before they are taken into her presence. If I am not at home, you are to refuse them admittance. There are to be no exceptions."

"Yes, my lord."

"Has anyone called for Mrs. Montgomery today?"

"Only the dressmaker and Mr. Browning."

"Browning? Already?"

"Mrs. Montgomery sent him a note this morning. Perhaps it was in response to that, my lord."

"A note? What . . . never mind. I will discuss it with her. Send a footman to see if Mrs. Montgomery feels well enough to join me in the library. I need to explain our new arrangements and warn her."

Lord Norwich strode toward the library, his head bowed, thoughts whirling in his brain. Things were happening so quickly he scarce had time to reason their meanings. He had gleaned several interesting things from his morning's outing with Lady Amabel and his conversation with Sir Harold, things that roused his suspicions mightily. But now he must deal with Allie before he could give time to such things.

Why had she summoned Browning? Was something wrong? Was she unhappy here? Did she have a tendre for Browning? For some inexplicable reason, the Earl found himself bristling at such an idea, searching for reasons to reject it.

When Allie entered the library, she was no longer distraught over the earlier occurrences, only concerned. Her worry increased, however, when she saw her brother-in-law. She had never spent much time around the male specimen, but the scowl on his face indicated a black mood. Rejecting the informality earlier decided upon between them, she said quietly, "You wanted to see me, my lord?"

"My lord? Are we no longer family?" Norwich snapped, frustration firing his anger.

"I was not sure. You looked so . . . so irritated, I did not want to upset you."

"I am only concerned with your well-being," he rapped out, the explosive force of his words causing Allie to retreat a step, bumping into a small table.

Her ensuing fluster gave Lord Norwich time to

pull himself together. As he began his own apology, however, Mrs. Montgomery also spoke, and courtesy demanded he give her the floor.

"I apologize for causing difficulties between you and your mother, Lord Norwich. I understand how difficult it is for you to have me here. I will move to a hotel as soon as Mavis has packed my belongings."

"Stepmother!" Lord Norwich explained between gritted teeth before continuing. "You will do no such thing. How am I to protect you if you are not here in my house? How would you manage on your own?"

"Mr. Browning has assured me I have all the funds I will need from my father's estate. He . . ."

"Funds! I am not speaking of money, woman! Why would Browning make such a statement? Does he not think I can care for my own family?"

Lord Norwich was by now in a towering rage, pacing back and forth across the library floor, his face dark with anger. Allie stared at her brother-in-law. "Perhaps you would like me to withdraw, my lord?" she asked soothingly.

The Earl whirled around to stare at her. "Withdraw? No! I would much prefer you explain what has been going on in my own house! Why did you write to Browning?"

"I am not a schoolgirl writing illicit notes, my lord," she responded frostily. "However, I will gladly inform you that I wrote to Mr. Browning to determine the state of my affairs. I had no wish to run up a large bill with Mme Feydeau that I could not pay."

"I told you I would take care of your wardrobe! Why can you not accept your role as a lady, a member of my family?"

"Because I am not a lady, my lord. I am a merchant's daughter!" Allie began her response in coldness, but she finished it in anger. She had heard that taunt from her unmourned husband, and it hurt even more coming from this man whom she had trusted and for whom she had even warmer feelings.

Her distress pierced his anger and he moved to her side to bring her hand to his lips. "I humbly beg your pardon, Allie. It has been a . . . difficult day, and I am greatly concerned for your safety."

"My safety? Whatever can you mean? I have been here all day in your house. What could happen to me here?"

"Please be seated." After escorting her to the sofa in front of the fireplace, Lord Norwich rang for tea. After it had been brought in, he allowed Allie to pour, and resumed his explanation. "I have had a rather interesting morning but have had little time to think through the events. But the concern for your safety arises from my stepmother. I'm sure you realize she is . . . unwell. She was never a calm person, high-strung, but today I . . . her emotions impressed me as dangerous."

Ruefully, Allie smiled. "Me too, my lord. I thought she was going to eat me whole."

Lord Norwich relaxed his grim visage slightly. "I am glad you were not too frightened, Allie, but

I feel we should take precautions against any
. . . any attempt to injure you."

"Surely your moth—stepmother would not go
so far as to do me harm now that she has calmed
down?"

"I do not think she has calmed down. I'm not
sure she will ever be able to think calmly again."
His eyes watched as Allie's color lessened, and
she nodded her head in agreement.

"Yes. Mavis said she had the look of a crazy
one!"

"Mavis is right. She is crazed with grief, and
she can be dangerous. She loved her son beyond
all reason."

Allie shuddered as she struggled to remember
anything lovable about the man she had married.
When she had first seen him in the church, perhaps he had seemed handsome, but she could not
really remember. The events following the wedding had obliterated any pleasant memories.

"I have given Jeffers instructions that anything
arriving for you must first be brought to my attention, and anyone calling on you must first be
interviewed by me."

"But you are putting yourself in danger for me,
John. I cannot allow that!"

"Allie, I am your protector. I must do so in
whatever way I can."

"But . . ."

"Am I supposed to throw open the door and
invite anyone in who wishes to do you harm?"

"No, of course not, but . . ."

"Allie, I am strong and able to defend myself.

If they are not seeking to injure me first, I will be prepared and they will not."

"You must keep several strong footmen close by at all times, John, to assist you."

Seeing her suggestion as an affront to his manhood, Norwich stiffened. "I am well able to care for myself, madam."

"John," Allie cried repentantly, "I did not mean to offend you. But . . . but I need you. I do not want anything to happen to you."

Norwich leaned forward to clasp her hands in his, a warm smile replacing the sternness. "Do not worry, Allie. I will take care of myself as well as you. I have no intention of hurrying my demise."

The entrance of Jeffers forced their withdrawal from such intimate conversation. Lord Norwich rose, irritated.

"Yes, Jeffers?"

"It is Mr. Browning, my lord. He says he must see you, that it is urgent."

"All right, Jeffers. Show him in here." What else has gone wrong this day, Lord Norwich wondered. Looking down at Allie, he debated whether he should send her away before Browning arrived, but he dismissed that idea. He wasn't sure she would obey him. She understood the "urgent matter" must have to do with her situation.

Mr. Browning entered and immediately realized no preliminaries were needed. As soon as the door had closed behind him, he began his explanation.

"Lord Norwich, Mrs. Montgomery, I went to

settle Mr. Tipton's estate this morning. While there, I decided to lay before the court Mr. Montgomery's estate, with the understanding that it depended upon the outcome of Mrs. Montgomery's trial. But it seems I was the second person interested in the estate." He paused, but no one spoke.

"A will has been brought to the court, one of which I had no prior knowledge. It seems that if Mrs. Montgomery dies within the next year, your brother's estate does not come to you, my lord, as I thought, but to someone else."

## *Chapter Six*

Only Lord Norwich seemed to see any significance in Mr. Browning's announcement. He frowned deeply, wondering what was coming next.

"Did he leave everything to his mother?" Allie asked.

"No, Mrs. Montgomery. He left it to a ne'er-do-well friend, whose name is—"

"Sir Harold Baynham."

The others turned to stare at Lord Norwich.

"You are correct, my lord," Mr. Browning said, "but how did you know?"

"I am finally putting some things together from my eventful morning."

"Did you gain information about Sir Harold? Do you think he is the murderer?" Mr. Browning asked eagerly.

"I don't know that I can condemn the man yet, but several things would point to that possibility."

"But what happened this morning?" Allie demanded impatiently.

"I called on Lady Amabel."

Allie bowed her head. She wasn't sure she wanted to hear of her brother-in-law's meeting with that woman.

"Did she tell you Sir Harold was guilty of . . . ?" she began.

"No, it will not be that simple. But . . . forgive me, Allie, but Lady Amabel and Sir Harold are most desirous that you hang. I could not understand such fervency, but this news explains it. Greed is a strong motivator."

"If they are both eager for . . . for my demise, does that mean they murdered Edward?" Allie asked in surprise.

"I doubt that Lady Amabel actually had a hand in the murder. But she is wearing full mourning everywhere this season to constantly remind the ton of Edward's death, and she says she will not leave off her mourning until you hang. She might be willing to assist Sir Harold in such a way."

"I think you've got something there. If all had gone according to plan," Mr. Browning added, "Mrs. Montgomery would have already hanged and her fortune transferred to Sir Harold with little notice. Though some might wonder where his sudden wealth came from, no one would suspect such a dastardly plan."

Allie sat quietly listening, a depression stealing in upon her. Her life, it seemed, was worth nothing more than a few gold coins. And not only her life. Her father had died because of what happened. Two lives sacrificed in order that these two members of the ton could live in the style to which they were accustomed.

"Allie?" Lord Norwich leaned toward the still woman, her luminous brown eyes sheltered from view. "Are you all right?"

"Yes, of course," she answered, without looking at her brother-in-law. "It is upsetting to realize how little my life is worth."

"My dear Allie," he assured her with a warm smile, "only to selfish, shallow people like those two."

Mr. Browning continued with a frown. "But while Lord Norwich and I *suspect* Sir Harold is the guilty party, we have no proof."

Allie spoke again, breaking into the silence that had fallen, "How do we get proof?"

No one had an answer to that essential question. Finally, Lord Norwich bestirred himself to say, "What we need is something to make him think we are on his trail. Perhaps he will then do something to hide what he thinks we have found and we can catch him."

"When you saw him this morning, did he have anything to say about Mrs. Montgomery living in your house?"

"Yes, Browning, he did become agitated when I told him, after Belle . . ."

"Belle! You are on such good terms with her?" Allie demanded before she could stop herself.

"She asked me to call her that, Allie." He did not see the pain and anger in her suddenly shuttered eyes and continued with his explanation. "When Belle left the room, he told me they were to be married, and I tried to use that fact to convince him Belle should give up wearing mourning. That was one of my main objectives in visiting her," he added with an air of sacrifice that was noticeably ignored by his sister-in-law. "But I had no success. He said she would continue to wear her weeds until Edward's murderer hanged. When I informed him that new evidence had turned up that indicated you might be innocent, he became very agitated."

"Hmmm, so he and Lady Amabel are to be married," Mr. Browning mused. "Perhaps they plotted to murder Montgomery together because her father cannot afford to give his daughter away to a worthless gamester like Baynham. He needs money too badly."

"But she is not going to wed Sir Harold," Norwich contradicted.

Allie, having been inexplicably relieved to hear that Lady Amabel was to be married, exclaimed, "But you just said . . ."

"I know but when I offered my felicitations to Lady Amabel, she assured me she was not engaged. She said her parents would not allow her to marry Sir Harold."

"Perhaps they are not yet aware that he expects to come into a large sum of money," Mr. Browning said.

"Or she refuses to commit herself until she is sure he will inherit," Allie muttered. "Why doesn't she just find someone else with a fortune to marry? After all, my husband did."

"My friends tell me she is almost beyond the pale. No man of substance would choose her when there are so many rich young ladies available. But what I cannot understand is why my brother would make Sir Harold his heir," puzzled Lord Norwich.

"There is always the possibility that the will is a forgery," Mr. Browning said hesitantly.

"That is true," Lord Norwich said consideringly.

"But what can we do to prove he killed my husband?" Allie demanded.

"Well, he is nervous about any new evidence, but it was clear this morning that he is entirely in Lady Amabel's pocket. She brought him to heel when he showed signs of panic."

"So, in order to frighten Sir Harold into revealing his guilt, we must remove him from Lady Amabel's influence, not an easy matter," Mr. Browning deduced.

All three studied the situation. Finally, Allie spoke up hesitantly. "If she is as you said, my lord, the best way to separate the two of them is to make her think the prize isn't worth the cost or . . . or to find her a better prize."

The other two stared at her, causing her to press back against her chair, before Lord Norwich exclaimed, "Brilliant, Allie! It is as if you were there this morning."

"What do you mean, my lord?" Mr. Browning demanded.

"Well, my intent was to tease Lady Amabel out of her ridiculous mourning . . . and to do so, I, uh, flirted with her." Allie frowned, causing his cravat to feel a little tight, but he continued. "And she responded with enthusiasm. It was after that that Sir Harold informed me they were to be married. So, the seeds of dissension have already been sown. It will be easy to widen the rift."

"No! I mean . . . it is not necessary for you to make such a sacrifice, surely," Allie protested.

"No, it is but a game," Browning cautioned, "and will be worth the effort if it sets you free."

Lord Norwich smiled wickedly. "Surely you do not think I would fall victim to Lady Amabel?"

"It would not be the first time, my lord, that a gentleman has been ensnared by a determined woman," Allie explained stiffly, hoping to hide her embarrassment.

Mr. Browning added his assurances. "While Lady Amabel is very beautiful, her true nature is such that Lord Norwich could not possibly fall under her spell."

"If our discussion is at an end, my lord," Allie said as she rose from the sofa, "I believe I shall retire to my room."

"Do you think Sir Harold will try to hasten Mrs. Montgomery's demise?" Mr. Browning asked when he and Norwich were alone.

"Ah, I forgot. You were not here when my stepmother arrived."

"Lady Norwich was here?"

"Yes, and I am afraid grief has left her unbalanced. She tried to injure Mrs. Montgomery and when I intervened, she issued some dire threats."

"This situation grows more complicated with each passing day."

"I understand Mrs. Montgomery sent for you this morning about some dressmaking bills."

Mr. Browning came to attention at the abrupt change of topic. "Yes, my lord."

"Those bills are mine. Pray charge them to my account."

"I'm sorry, my lord, but Mrs. Montgomery has already given me instructions regarding those bills."

"Damn it, man, you are my man of business! You will do as I say!"

Mr. Browning straightened his shoulders and brushed his blond hair back from his face, prepared to face the challenge inherent in Lord Norwich's words. "I am also employed by Mrs. Montgomery, my lord. Would you have me go against her orders?"

"I engaged Mme Feydeau. Therefore, I should . . ."

"Lord Norwich, Mrs. Montgomery is already residing under your roof. Do you not see how much better it will appear if she pays for her own clothes? After all, her father's estate is quite large, even after the dowry he provided your brother."

"I suppose the gossips would— How large is her father's estate . . . that is, if you feel Mrs. Montgomery wouldn't mind your revealing that information."

"Approximately thirty thousand pounds a

year, more or less. It depends upon whether or
not she keeps her father's factories or sells out
and puts the proceeds in the funds."

"That is an impressive figure. Combined with
her person, she will have many suitors after her
year of mourning has passed."

"Yes, I suppose she will," Mr. Browning
agreed, eyeing his employer speculatively,
"though I'm not sure how receptive she will be
after her experience with your brother."

"There is no need for her to marry if she does
not wish it. She may remain under my roof as
long as she desires."

"That is kind of you, my lord. But when you
marry, will not your wife prefer her removal?"

"I? I . . . may never marry. There is a cousin
to inherit, certainly a better candidate for my es-
tates than my late brother."

Allie, after leaving the two men in the library,
returned to her room to stare broodingly out the
window. The threat of hanging was receding each
day as she enjoyed the freedom and luxury of her
present situation. But that fear was being re-
placed by both a healthy curiosity about the
world to which her marriage had raised her and
now the irritant of Lady Amabel.

Though she hastened to remind herself that her
brother-in-law was free to socialize with any
woman of his choice, the fact that he had chosen
Lady Amabel was upsetting. She had to remind
herself again and again that he was only doing
his duty. But he had become the center of her

universe in a few short days. His presence quickened her heart in spite of herself.

She had difficulty hiding the jealousy Lady Amabel provoked in her. That jealousy brought an overwhelming curiosity about the woman who had been a part of the horrible hoax of her marriage. She was determined to see the woman whose beauty had even been noted by the steadfast Mr. Browning.

Moving over to face herself in the beveled glass, Allie studied her somber figure with distaste. Though her eyes were large and had a luxurious fringe of dark lashes, they were a soft brown, not the blue eyes favored by the ton this season. And her brown hair, in its sensible plait pinned at the nape of her slender neck, did nothing to flatter her thin face. At least her skin was no longer so pasty, since she had left the prison. Good food and rest had had their effect. But she recognized sadly that she would be unable to compete with an acknowledged Beauty as Lady Amabel was reputed to be.

Compete? Realization of where her thoughts were again leading her caused Allie to turn from her reflection. Of course she was not competing with Lady Amabel. But there was no reason, she resolved firmly, not to look her best. She would send a note to Mme Feydeau immediately, asking for the name of a hairdresser to transform her plait into one of the styles favored by the ton. Then, when her wardrobe was delivered, she could at least have Lord Norwich's groom drive her through the park and perhaps do some shopping. And, if by chance, she looked for one particular person among the fashionables to be seen there, who would know?

Allie's heart fluttered when she received word from Jeffers that Lord Norwich was expecting her to join him at dinner that evening.

"Oh, Mavis, if only I had one of my new gowns. All I have to wear is that awful black bombazine that is five years old."

"Maybe I can do your hair in a special way, Allie. I'm very good with hair."

"Would you, Mavis? That would be wonderful!"

"Why don't I order a bath for you and we'll wash your hair. Then you can relax before the fire on the chaise longue while I dry it and tie it up."

Though Allie followed her friend's directions, she was no calmer when it was time to descend to dinner. Just the thought of being in Lord Norwich's presence caused a delicious tingle down her spine, something she had never before experienced.

"Good evening, Allie," the distinguished, dark-haired man said.

Perhaps it was his voice, Allie considered, even as she curtsied. Those deep, velvety tones seemed to caress her very being. "Good evening, John."

"I trust you suffered no distress from your busy day?"

"No. I must again thank you for sending Mme Feydeau to me. I can't wait to wear pretty colors."

A warm smile lit up his face. "I'm sure you will

look delightful, my dear, but I have nothing to complain about this evening."

Allie's cheeks suffused with color as she took his extended arm to enter the dining room. "Thank you." She fought the urge to pat the complicated coils of hair Mavis had worked on for an hour.

Once dinner was under way, Lord Norwich launched into an innocuous discussion of books Allie had enjoyed, hoping to put his sister-in-law at ease. As she grew more and more relaxed, Lord Norwich discovered how pleasant it was to have feminine companionship at his evening meal. The candlelight reflected off her delicate features and her soft voice was as soothing to his ears as the most beautiful music.

"John? John, I asked if you thought we were any closer to discovering who killed Edward?"

"Sorry, Allie, I was distracted. Yes, I think we are on the right track, but I would not expect . . . that is, I do not want you to think this will be easily accomplished."

"I know, John. What are you going to do next?"

John looked into her sweet face and wished he could present her her freedom on a silver platter. She was too gentle and good to have been accused in the first place. With frustration, he said, "All I can do this evening is stay near Lady Amabel and Sir Harold and try to make them uneasy."

"May I accompany you?"

"Allie, I think it best if you did not just yet." He could scarce bear the disappointment in her eyes. "After your new gowns have arrived, perhaps you might visit some museums, or . . . or shop . . . or something."

"Yes, of course," she said, her voice drained of its earlier animation.

Lord Norwich was unaware they had reached the end of the meal, but Allie's rising signaled their time together was over. He arose and stared down at her. With a finger beneath her chin, he lifted her face. "Sweet Allie, please, trust me. I want to protect you . . . and prove you innocent, but I . . . I am no miracle worker."

Allie looked up into his blue eyes and forced a smile to her lips. "I know. I'll try to be patient. And I believe you will succeed, John. I *do* have faith in you."

Her earnestness touched Norwich and he unconsciously drew closer, his eyes trained on her soft lips.

His nearness stole Allie's breath as she inhaled his masculine scent and for the first time in her life, she felt drawn to a man, a special man. She waited eagerly for her first kiss.

"Will there be anything else, my lord?" Jeffers asked as he entered from his pantry.

Lord Norwich stepped back from his sister-in-law and said huskily, "No, no, Jeffers. Unless Mrs. Montgomery wants tea in the drawing room."

"No, I believe I shall just go to my room. The dinner was excellent, Jeffers. Please give Cook my compliments."

With a hurried curtsy to her companion, Allie sped from the room, her cheeks aflame. She had made a fool of herself, she knew, standing there, her behavior begging him to kiss her. Her aunt would have put her on bread and water for a month for such forward behavior.

Lord Norwich watched Allie leave the dining room, his mind dwelling on the past moment, before he realized what he had been about to do. How could he even think of taking advantage of her innocence? He was sworn to protect his sister-in-law and yet he had intended to . . . no, wanted to taste the softness of her lips, to caress . . . he shook himself. He must put such thoughts totally from his mind. Allie trusted him. And he would not betray her trust.

He stalked from the dining room, resigned to an evening in the company of Lady Amabel, but his heart remained upstairs with Allie.

"What is it now, Jeffers?" Lord Norwich asked with impatience as his butler once again intruded on his private domain. He had been working all morning on papers concerning his various holdings, long neglected during his travels and his activities on behalf of Mrs. Montgomery. His progress, however, had been slow due to the constant interruptions brought on by his orders from the day before.

There had been several deliveries from Mme Feydeau to his sister-in-law, each of which had to be inspected, including a collection of silken undergarments, for Mrs. Montgomery's safety. But he hoped that was the last of such deliveries. He found the image of Allie in such garments to

be even more disturbing than the interruptions
. . . and more difficult to forget.

Next there was a hairdresser to be interviewed,
a small man with a mincing gait and a strong lav-
ender scent. He had had to request confirmation
from Allie that she had actually sent for such a
creature. No sooner was that gentleman ascend-
ing the main staircase than a delivery from a boot
maker was brought into the library, followed
closely by several hatboxes from Mme Sophie's
shop on Bond Street. Only the hate visible in his
stepmother's eyes had kept him from ordering
them all to depart from his presence at once. Now
it seemed there was yet another interruption with
which to deal.

"My lord, Lord Caston is here to see you."

"Show him in," the Earl replied, shoving his
papers away. It was fruitless to continue his efforts. He rose as his friend entered the library.
"Caston, what brings you here?"

With a lift of his brows, Lord Caston responded, "Must I have a reason for calling on an
old friend?"

Lord Norwich grinned. "Of course not. I will
reward you for your efforts with a glass of sherry,
friend. Come sit down."

After serving himself and his guest, Lord Norwich listened to Caston's chatter about the social
events of the season. Pausing to take a sip of his
drink, Caston swirled the liquid around the cut-
crystal goblet as he said casually, "I saw you last
evening at Lady Mayberry's dangling after Lady
Amabel. Quite a Beauty."

"Yes," Lord Norwich agreed pleasantly.

"She was quite visible in her black."

"Yes."

"It was frequently, uh, noticed that you were in her pocket all evening."

"Really?"

"Some people were rather surprised at your choice of companion."

"Oh?"

"Norwich! What is going on?"

"Ah," Lord Norwich answered with a grin, "you mean this call had a purpose after all? You are not simply here to assure me of the depth of our friendship?"

"Norwich," Lord Caston repeated warningly.

"All right, Caston, no need to become uppity. I suppose I must be grateful that you did not assume I was captivated by the lady's beauty. I'm sure that is what most of the ton is saying this morning."

"Well, yes, which is one of the reasons I came."

"And the other?"

"To satisfy my own curiosity," Lord Caston assured him with a grin, "and to offer my assistance if needed."

"Thank you, Caston. I wish there were something you could do. I'm not even sure what I am trying to accomplish. Originally, I had hoped to flatter the lady into abandoning her conspicuous mourning. Then . . . this must go no further," Lord Norwich cautioned, "something occurred that drew my attention to her admirer, Sir Harold. When he expressed jealousy, I thought to pursue the lady in hopes of rattling the enemy."

"And have you succeeded?"

"Not to the extent I had hoped. His jealous eyes never left us, but he made no unwise utterances."

"You think he knows who killed Edward?"

"If he did not commit the deed himself."

"But he is a gentleman! Surely . . ."

"Come, Caston, my brother alone should have convinced you there are gentlemen without honor. He certainly did so for Mrs. Montgomery."

"Yes, I suppose so. How is your . . . Mrs. Montgomery faring?"

"As well as can be expected. She is recovering from her ordeal in the prison, but, of course, she is living under difficult circumstances."

As if to give lie to the sad figure he had described, the library door opened, revealing a charming lady in pale lilac, soft curls framing her face, and a delightful smile on her lips.

"John! What do you . . . Oh! Please forgive me. I did not know you were occupied." Allie, her cheeks flushed in embarrassment, tried to escape but was halted by both gentlemen.

"Please do not depart on my account," Lord Caston begged, admiration in his eyes.

"Come in, Allie," Lord Norwich added, though with less enthusiasm than his friend. He was stunned by the change in her appearance. She seemed to have turned into a blushing beauty overnight, and he wasn't sure of the wisdom of presenting his sister-in-law to his friend . . . at least not yet. Now, of course, he had no choice.

"Mrs. Montgomery, allow me to present to you

a very dear friend, Lord Caston. Caston, my sister-in-law, Mrs. Montgomery."

Lord Caston moved forward to take Allie's small hand in his and lift it to his lips. "I am delighted to meet you, madam."

Despite her embarrassment, Allie's strict upbringing allowed her to regain her composure. "Thank you, my lord. I am pleased to meet any friend of my brother-in-law."

As Lord Caston led Allie to the sofa with the intent of engaging her in social chatter to better their acquaintance, Lord Norwich intervened with an abruptness that surprised even him. "You wanted to see me, madam?"

Disturbed by his stern tone and hurt that he had expressed no pleasure over her changed appearance, Allie withdrew her hand from Lord Caston's, her cheeks red. "I wanted to . . . it is of no matter. I will ask later," she finished in confusion as both men stared at her.

"If I can be of service to you, please, your request is my command," Lord Caston immediately offered.

"Nay, Caston, Mrs. Montgomery is my responsibility. I will provide for her needs," Lord Norwich inserted hurriedly before Allie could respond.

Though she was not pleased at being termed a "responsibility," Allie explained, "John . . . Lord Norwich, all I wished for was the use of your carriage for a ride through the park now that I am presentable." She added anxiously, "I could not bring myself to wear black, but lilac is considered half mourning, and I would like to see something of London while I may."

While Lord Norwich wrestled between his desire to please Mrs. Montgomery and the wisdom of exposing her to the ton, his friend stepped in.

"My carriage is at the door, Mrs. Montgomery. I would be delighted if you would allow me to escort you through the park. It is a lovely day for a drive."

"I . . . I would be honored, Lord Caston, if it is all right with Lord Norwich?"

Unable to articulate his reluctance, Norwich shrugged. "Whatever is your pleasure, my dear."

"Then I would love to drive in the park with you, my lord." Allie accepted Caston's invitation with a smile and a sidelong look at Lord Norwich. "I will fetch a wrap and bonnet and return in a moment, my lord, if you do not mind."

After watching her trim figure depart, Lord Caston turned back to his friend. "Your sister-in-law is charming, Norwich."

"Yes, but I am not sure it is wise to expose her to the ton, at this time."

"Just a ride through the park, Norwich. I will take care of her."

Norwich's uneasiness persisted in spite of his friend's assurances, and he stood staring into the flickering flames in the fireplace after their departure. Suppose they met his stepmother in the park? Would she recognize Mrs. Montgomery? The widow's looks were certainly improved. She gave the impression of a fragile flower, her large brown eyes soft and inviting. Caston had certainly been willing to do whatever she wished, he thought in irritation.

With a shake of his head, Lord Norwich drew his mind back to the subject at hand. Perhaps he himself had better join the day's promenade, just as a precaution, he assured himself, as he rang for Jeffers to order his favorite mount brought to the front door.

Allie was put completely at ease by her companion's gentle, undemanding conversation, leaving her free to take in the sights and sounds of London. The bustling activity thrilled her. When they turned into the confines of Hyde Park, Allie was surprised to find almost as much traffic there as in the London streets.

"It is like this every day, Mrs. Montgomery," Lord Caston explained. "Everyone comes to see and be seen. The most illustrious of the ton and the most determined hangers-on mingle here."

"Oh! Look, that gentleman has a little dog beside him."

"That is Poodle Byng. He never goes anywhere without his little dog."

"And the lady in the pink carriage?"

"Oh, um, well, that is someone beneath your notice," Lord Caston assured her, directing her lingering eyes away from the Cyprian who was already attended by several young bucks. As they rounded the next turn slowly, ignoring the curious stares of those driving past them, Allie spotted a beautiful young woman dressed totally in black. She did not need to ask her identity.

When Lord Caston saw in what direction his

companion's attention was drawn, he determined it would be in his best interest to direct Mrs. Montgomery's view in another direction. He was further assured of that when he recognized one of her escorts. Unfortunately, Mrs. Montgomery recognized the gentleman also.

"Lord Norwich is with that woman."

"Yes . . . well . . . I suppose he felt the need of exercise. Over there you can see . . ." Lord Caston began but stopped when he realized she was ignoring his attempts to distract her. Small beads of perspiration broke out on his forehead at the realization that the two vehicles would soon draw even with each other.

## Chapter Seven

Lord Norwich had entered the park only minutes after his sister-in-law and her escort, his mount moving more easily through London's crowded streets. But he had only gone a short distance when he was hailed to the side of Lady Amabel. With a guarded look around him, Lord Norwich greeted the lady warmly.

"Lady Amabel, lovely as always."

"John, I had hoped to receive you this morning," the lady greeted him, leaning toward him in another of her low-cut black bombazine gowns.

Damn, did the woman own no decent gowns,

Lord Norwich wondered as he tried to briefly kiss her hand. Her clinging fingers and fluttering lashes forestalled his withdrawal. "I had paperwork to do, my lady."

"Pooh! Sad stuff," Lady Amabel pouted. "You will accompany me now, to make up for your neglect," she ordered imperiously. "Harry, you must walk for a while and I will pick you up again after Lord Norwich has taken a turn with me."

"No, Belle! This is my rig! I ain't letting you nor his lordship drive it!"

"I would not hear of such, Sir Harold," Norwich hastily assured him. "I will ride along beside you a little way, my lady."

"Very well," Lady Amabel acceded, "but you will have to make it up to me later."

"I am always at your service, Belle," Norwich assured her just as he caught sight of his friend and Mrs. Montgomery approaching. With a silent groan he turned back to distract Lady Amabel.

One of the hangers-on, however, foiled his efforts. "Lord Caston has found a new bird. I wonder if she has a fortune. Not that Caston has a need for one," the man snorted in disgust, "but blunt does call to blunt. Perhaps I'll see if I can wangle an introduction. She's not a diamond but pretty enough if there's money."

"Is Caston not a friend of yours, John?" Lady Amabel inquired eagerly. "Why not introduce him to me. I would like to meet the so very proper Lord Caston."

Norwich recognized Lady Amabel's challenge,

but his quandary was not in presenting Lord Caston to the lady but his companion. He could rely only on Lady Amabel's good manners, a shaky support at best.

"Certainly, my lady, if you wish it, but . . ."

The tension in his voice alerted Lady Amabel, and she eyed Lord Caston's companion more carefully, but she saw no potential rival in that drab little creature.

Lord Caston was hailed by Mr. William Hastings and he pulled his horses to a stop in great relief. Now if only Lord Norwich could maneuver his party past while they were engaged in conversation with Billy . . .

"Mrs. Montgomery, may I present a close friend to both myself and Lord Norwich, Mr. William Hastings?"

Allie shyly extended her hand, a smile on her lips.

"Billy, this is Mrs. Montgomery, Norwich's sister-in-law."

"Pleasure, madam. Norwich is lucky to have such a charming addition to his family."

"Thank you, sir, you are so kind."

While pleasantries were being exchanged, Lord Caston kept an unobtrusive watch on Lady Amabel's approaching carriage and outriders. He would not have chosen such an occurrence to enliven his day, but he saw Lord Norwich was unable to avoid it.

Allie, too, was aware of the approach of Lord Norwich and Lady Amabel, and she found herself a mixture of emotions. Jealousy was in the forefront, both of the woman's obvious beauty and her brother-in-law's presence in her entourage. But there was also anger.

This woman, so eager to see her hang, had conspired to rob her of her dowry and hastened her father's demise. Allie's shoulders stiffened and her chin rose as her blond foe smiled flirtatiously at Caston and Hastings, ignoring her completely.

Lord Norwich, accepting the hand Fate dealt him, moved his horse forward to make the presentations Lady Amabel thought she so greatly desired. Casting a warning look at his two friends, he began, "Lady Amabel, may I present two friends, Lord Caston and Mr. Hastings, and . . . Mrs. Montgomery, my brother's widow."

Lady Amabel, in the process of bestowing flirtatious smiles on the two highly eligible gentlemen, stiffened as his final words penetrated. Her smile froze.

Both gentlemen ignored the tense silence and acknowledged the introduction with perfunctory nods while all eyes focused on the two women, awaiting their reactions. It was Mrs. Montgomery who won the day, as much to her surprise as to the others. Staring straight ahead, she allowed her anger free rein as she said, "I refuse to be presented to such an unprincipled woman. May we move on, my lord?"

Fortunately, Lord Caston was not one of those paralyzed by his companion's response and by the time Lady Amabel recovered, Caston's carriage was well away from the encounter, followed closely by Mr. Hastings. Not so far away, however, that Mrs. Montgomery could not enjoy the scream of rage that rose from the center of the crowd they left behind.

By the time Lord Caston, Mrs. Montgomery, and Mr. Hastings returned to Lord Norwich's house, word of their encounter had flown round Hyde Park and spread into the stately salons of the city.

The notorious widow's stock among society's matrons had risen considerably. Lady Amabel had long been a thorn in the side of those who determined the by-laws of the exclusive club called the ton, and none had been as successful as Mrs. Montgomery at putting her in her place.

In her family, however, Mrs. Montgomery had lost ground, as she discovered quite easily while pouring tea for her two guests. Both gentlemen had quite willingly entered Lord Norwich's parlor and accepted the offer of tea, eager to become better acquainted with the charming Mrs. Montgomery. When she attempted to apologize for what had happened, it was Mr. Hastings who reassured her.

"No need to apologize, ma'am. Norwich shouldn't have presented her to you. Besides, when one apologizes, it makes everyone think you're wrong."

"Yes, but perhaps I was . . . rude."

"No, Billy has the right of it. You could not acknowledge the woman."

Allie's attempt to express her gratitude for their support was halted by the eruption into the parlor of her outraged brother-in-law. "There you are, madam!" he shouted.

Billy's matter-of-fact response, "Where else would she be, Norwich?" rather took the wind out of the Earl's sails.

"I'm not sure . . . perhaps planning her next attempt to undo all my hard work!"

"Norwich, you must not talk like that," Caston warned, a frown on his brow as he saw Mrs. Montgomery turn pale.

"John," Allie began composedly, pleading for his understanding, "I could not bring myself to acknowledge the woman. Wrapping herself in the willow, she flaunts her relationship with my husband and makes no secret that she wants me to hang for his murder!"

"You could have—have nodded, or something, without giving her the cut complete!"

"No, I could not!" Allie shouted back, her anger rising as he continued to defend Lady Amabel. "Not even for you will I be so hypocritical! She knew about my husband's plan to bilk me of my dowry. Knew of it and approved! Now she campaigns for my death! I *will not* greet her!"

All three men stared in surprise at the raging form before them, her delicate appearance having given no indication of the depths beneath. When silence followed her ringing declaration, realization of her behavior struck Allie and her cheeks flooded crimson. Covering her face with her hands, she sank back onto the sofa.

Lord Norwich, both bewildered by Allie's reaction and uneasily aware of his gaffe in presenting Lady Amabel, sought retreat. He had no desire to face either his friends or the not-so-fragile female now occupying his house. Without a word, he stomped to the door of the parlor and shut it behind him. At the sound, Allie raised her woebegone face from her hands.

"Here now," Billy pleaded nervously, "no need for tears. You are perfectly right. Norwich was wrong to present that nasty female."

"Thank you, Mr. Hastings, but I fear his lordship does not agree with you."

"Now that is where you are wrong," Caston assured her warmly, moving beside her on the sofa and taking her hand in his. "Norwich is perfectly aware he brought the entire disaster down upon his own head. He should have expected nothing else. It is because he feels guilty that he did not remain. It is unpleasant to admit when one is wrong."

"Are you sure, my lord?" Allie asked anxiously, mopping her eyes delicately with a handkerchief supplied by Mr. Hastings. "I owe him so much. I would have died in Newgate, you know, if he had not obtained my release." Her eyes closed momentarily as she thought back to those horrible days. "Perhaps I should have . . . I do not want to displease him, but I could not . . ."

"Of course not. And he was wrong to expect you to," Caston assured her. "He will realize it, my dear. It—it may take him a little time."

"Oh, I hope so."

"Must appear in public again at once."

The pronouncement from Mr. Hastings had the other two staring at him in confusion. "What is that, Billy?" Lord Caston demanded.

"Mrs. Montgomery must appear in public again as soon as possible. Only way to assure the ton she is above reproach and Lady Amabel is the villainess."

"You are right, Mr. Hastings," Allie said firmly after a minute's consideration. "And I would like to do what I can to prove the woman wrong. But Lord Norwich would never agree."

"He will, when we explain it," Billy assured her in no-nonsense terms.

"Billy, I'm not sure . . ." Lord Caston began.

"Well, I am. I know how the tongues work. You scored a victory this afternoon, Mrs. Montgomery. Lady Amabel is not liked . . . well, except by some of the men. But they don't count. It's the rulers of the ton that count, and they don't like Lady Amabel. Now, where . . . ah! The theater! We'll take Mrs. Montgomery to the theater this evening. Take my sister along. Nice lady, you'll like her."

"I would love to go if you can convince Lord Norwich."

"Mrs. Montgomery, I am coming to think you and Billy may have something there. If you appear this evening, all properly dressed, they will recognize your quality and come down heavily on your side," Lord Caston determined. "And you will want them on your side when all this is resolved."

"Do you think Lord Norwich will approve?" Allie asked, determined to participate in her own rescue.

"We will handle Norwich, madam. Don't

worry about him. Do you as yet have something proper to wear to the theater?"

"Yes, I ordered several things from Mme Feydeau that should do if they have been delivered."

"Ah, Mme Feydeau. Excellent! You write her a note if they are not yet here and demand one of them at once. Do you have any jewels?" Billy questioned earnestly, surprising Allie.

"Jewels? Why, no, I . . ."

"Talk to Norwich about that."

"I could not . . ."

"He means we will talk to Norwich, Mrs. Montgomery. You should have received some jewels by now. If it has not occurred to Norwich, we will remedy that."

"I truly appreciate your assistance, gentlemen. I believe the only way to prove Lady Amabel wrong is to confront her."

"What colors are your dresses?"

Billy's single-mindedness surprised Allie.

"Why—why, one is a soft gray and the other is a paler shade of lilac. I felt I should show some respect for Mr. Montgomery's death."

"Exactly right. Choose the gray for this evening. We will advise Norwich diamonds," he decided.

"But are you sure you can convince him?"

"It is all right, Mrs. Montgomery, I assure you. If Billy says diamonds, then diamonds it is. And together we'll convince Norwich. Now, you must hurry and prepare yourself for an evening at the theater."

Ushered from the parlor, Mrs. Montgomery ascended the stairs in thoughtful silence. The support of the two gentlemen had done much to soothe the agitation brought on by her confrontation in Hyde Park. And she knew without their support, Lord Norwich would never agree to the evening's entertainment. She raised her chin in determination. She did not want him to be angry with her, but she would not let that woman think she was afraid to face her. Perhaps his friends could make him see reason.

The two conspirators for Mrs. Montgomery's social launching exchanged a look when they were ushered into Lord Norwich's library. That gentleman was standing with his back to them, staring out the window. He made no move to greet his friends or to even acknowledge their presence.

"Norwich? We need to discuss something with you," Lord Caston said hesitantly, hoping to discover some encouraging sign that his friend was not still angry.

"If you are come to defend Mrs. Montgomery's behavior, you are wasting your time," he intoned, keeping his back to them.

"Here now, Norwich, nothing to argue about there. She did the right thing," Mr. Hastings assured him, his mind on the next step in their little puzzle. "What we've got to . . ."

"What? She did the right thing?" Lord Norwich roared. "I've been cultivating Amabel Courtney, hoping to find a way to prove that chit's innocence, and she destroys it all in a split second of pride!"

"Stands to reason," Billy replied calmly. "Even if you flirt with the woman, it doesn't mean you would want your family to consort with her. Woman's beyond the pale. Wouldn't present her to my sister."

"I know that, Billy. I didn't want . . . but I was trapped. Lady Amabel wanted to up her social status by being introduced to the two of you. She didn't know whom Giles was escorting. But now she is furious. I doubt she'll ever even acknowledge me, much less take me into her confidence."

"Don't see why not. You have no control over Mrs. Montgomery's behavior. Well, I mean, that's obvious. Tell her it has nothing to do with your feelings."

The other two men stared at Mr. Hastings until he began to fidget, wondering if his starched cravat had wilted.

"Now why didn't I think of that? The beautiful thing about it is that it is the truth . . . at least, the first part is. Thank you, Billy," Lord Norwich enthused as he moved forward to shake his friend's hand. "That's exactly what I will do. I'll send flowers this very day with my card and make sure I see her this evening."

"Good idea, Norwich, and while we're on the subject of this evening, uh, Billy and I—well, really Billy and Mrs. Montgomery—had an idea."

Norwich studied Caston carefully. It was unusual to see his friend ill at ease or unsure of himself, but he was demonstrating such now, while Billy, easily disturbed, was concentrating on something and seemed in total control. His curiosity roused, Lord Norwich said, "Why don't we be seated. I can tell you have something on your mind."

Once settled, Caston searched in vain for a diplomatic way to explain their plan, but an impatient Hastings blurted, "It's this way, Norwich. Mrs. Montgomery scored a victory over Lady Amabel today and that will stand her in good stead with the ton. What we need to do now is ease her into society. Otherwise, they'll think she ain't presentable. So we . . ."

"You mean introduce her? But the chit's accused of murder!" He shook his head. "Has everyone around me gone mad?"

"You're mistaken, my boy," Mr. Hastings assured him. "We expect you to prove she's innocent. Meanwhile, we thought we'd escort her to the theater this evening, along with my sister, of course. Casually present her to a few people, nothing pushy, but they'll all see she's gently bred. The way Edward kept her stashed away in Half Moon Street, no wonder there have been all sorts of strange rumors about the woman he married. Most of the ton expect her to have hay in her hair! They will be pleasantly surprised to see that she's a fine lady."

"That's true," Lord Norwich agreed, his mind reviewing Mr. Hastings's plan for unforeseen difficulties. He hated the idea of sharing her—introducing her to other eligible men. "You may be right, Billy. She is certainly presentable and it would be as well if the ton knows that as soon as possible. Will she consider going? Have you discussed this with her?"

"She's worried about your reaction," Lord Caston informed him. "You cut up pretty stiff with her."

"Yes, I know. I suppose I owe her an apology," Lord Norwich admitted with a reluctant sigh, "but—"

Jeffers rapped smartly on the door, cutting off Lord Norwich's remark. "Yes, Jeffers?"

"Another delivery for Mrs. Montgomery, sir. Shall I have them bring it in here?"

With his mind on weightier matters and because of the presence of his two friends, Lord Norwich ignored his earlier plan and dismissed the butler with instructions to have the delivery taken directly up to Mrs. Montgomery. It was Mr. Hastings's intervention that changed his directions.

"No, we must see if it is the dress for this evening. Must be sure it will be appropriate."

"Billy, I can assure you Mrs. Montgomery will be properly attired—" Lord Norwich began but was interrupted by the other man.

"Also need to discuss jewelry with you. Have them bring it in here, man," Billy ordered the butler.

Lord Norwich protested but gave in to his friend's demanding look. "Oh, all right, Jeffers, have them bring it in here."

Once his employer had confirmed Mr. Hastings's orders, Jeffers bowed himself out to execute them. A moment later, the door opened and Jeffers entered again, followed by a footman carrying several pristine white boxes from Mme Feydeau. Jeffers indicated the man should place them on a table near Lord Norwich and then escorted the footman from the room, closing the door quietly behind them.

The three men looked at the boxes and then at each other, an awkwardness stealing upon them. Finally Billy moved toward the largest.

"Nothing personal, you know, but must see if I was right about the diamonds. You do have diamonds she can wear this evening, don't you, Norwich? I mean, family necklace or something? Can't have her going about like a penniless orphan."

"Yes, of course, there are several diamond necklaces, rings, bracelets, any of which she may wear. I had not thought . . ." Lord Norwich stopped as Billy drew the lid from the box to reveal what seemed to be acres of diaphanous gray silk.

"Ah, perfect. The perfect color. Shows respect for the dead without deep mourning."

"But he was her husband. Are you sure the ton will accept . . ."

"Don't matter, Caston. Everyone knows what he was about. Won't think any less of her for not wearing black. Besides, someone else is already wearing that. Don't want to look like her."

"No, of course not."

Billy leaned forward to lift the dress from its wrappings, his eyes studying the line and cut. "Attractive without being immodest," he announced. "That Feydeau woman knows her stuff. This will be . . . Here now! What's this brown —*agh!*"

Billy's gasp took the other two by surprise.

They both drew curiously closer as all color drained from Billy's face.

"Billy, what is it? Do you feel unwell?" Caston asked, moving to his friend, while Norwich followed the direction of Billy's shaking finger and looked at the gown.

A slight movement among the diaphanous gray folds caught his attention. It became riveted when something slithered across the silk. He grabbed a fire iron from beside the mantel and inched toward the gown lying partially in the box. "What is it, Billy? As asp?" he whispered. "Some type of snake?"

"Yes . . . an asp! Damned thing . . . I almost picked it up."

"How can I help, John?" Lord Caston asked, voice soft, body perfectly still.

"Find a weapon. There! Billy, give the dress a shake and flush out the beast. We must not let it escape."

In a matter of moments, it was over. Billy's swift shaking of the gown dumped the small but deadly snake on the Aubusson carpet, and Lord Norwich pounced at once with his fire iron, smashing the life out of it.

All three men stood in silence, staring at the remains.

"Indeed, someone wants Mrs. Montgomery dead!" Lord Caston exhaled.

"Your own lives will be at risk if you accompany her."

"This is monstrous!" Billy protested, outraged. "Cowardly! No gentleman could turn his back on a lady in such distress!"

Norwich smiled. Hastings was thought to be the least daring of the three, but he proved himself stout of heart. "Thank you, Billy."

Still shaken, Mr. Hastings muttered, "You do have your hands full, old boy. Well, I just wanted to check the color. Diamonds is what she needs. You'll see to it, Norwich?" At his friend's nod, Mr. Hastings turned toward the door. "Don't feel so well . . . think I'll be toddling 'long."

Caston and Norwich exchanged slight smiles before Caston followed their friend, a supportive arm under his. "I'll accompany you, Billy. Stop by my place. It's nearer. We'll have a brandy to celebrate our heroics." He said over his shoulder, "We will return this evening to escort Mrs. Montgomery to the theater."

Before Lord Norwich ascended the stairs to offer an apology to his sister-in-law, he had a stiff drink, along with Jeffers and the footman who, alarmed by the commotion, arrived not a moment too soon to staunchly carry the loathsome object away from the library to the dustbin before it was discovered by an unsuspecting maid.

Lord Norwich rapped on the door. When Mavis opened it, he said awkwardly, "Mavis, is Mrs. Montgomery available? I need to speak with her."

There was a whispered conversation that grated on his nerves before Allie appeared at the door. She said nothing, only stared up at him with big eyes.

"Allie, I've come to offer my apologies."

With relief, Allie moved toward him, extending hands that he quickly clasped. "Oh, my lord. I too am sorry. I truly did not mean to cause any difficulty. It was just that I could not . . ."

"I know. And you were in the right of it." He paused as a chambermaid scurried by, looking at them out of the corner of her eye, making him feel like a schoolboy caught with his hand in the cookie jar. "I agree with Billy's plan for the theater this evening. He approved of the gray silk and I am to send up diamonds."

"Oh, please, I do not need . . ."

"But we are under strict orders, my dear. I would not dare disobey Billy. Besides, they'll suit you." She blushed, but before she could speak, he added softly, "Thank you for so generously forgiving me, Allie. I will see you at dinner." He unexpectedly bent down and kissed her cheek, then turned and hurried down the hallway. Allie stood looking after him, her hand cradling her warm face.

"Oh, my, you're beautiful!" Mavis gasped as she smoothed down the silvery gray skirt.

Allie stared at herself in the looking glass, unable to believe that the elegantly dressed young woman reflected there was herself. "It is a wonderful gown."

"It's not just the gown. *You* look wonderful this evening."

"I suspect it is the excitement, Mavis. I have never been to a real theater before."

There was a knock at the door, startling both women. Mavis crossed to the door and discovered an impatient Lord Norwich there. "I've come to bring the required diamonds," he explained as his eyes sought out Allie.

"Come in, John. It is kind of you to deliver them personally," Allie said with a smile.

"I have an ulterior motive, I must confess. I wanted to have a word with you."

Mavis moved toward the other door. "I will be in the next room if you need further assistance."

Before turning to Lord Norwich, Allie watched her abigail leave the room. Then she said expectantly, "Yes, John?"

"Allie, I know you are in favor of the plans for this evening, but I feel it necessary to warn you of the dangers."

Sighing with disappointment, she turned from him and stared into the mirror. "Perhaps there will be some danger, but I am glad I am going out. Do you know she is saying wicked things about me? Mr. Hastings said people think I am unfit for society."

"They will have no doubts after this evening, Allie. You look charming. But that does not eliminate the possibility of your being harmed."

"Surely Lady Amabel would not . . ."

"You must be very careful."

"Yes, of course. I wish you could accompany us this evening."

Lord Norwich took her hand and raised it to his lips, murmuring, "I too wish I could be with you."

The world faded from view as they gazed at each other, each committing the sweet moment to memory. A noise in the hallway jarred Norwich from his reverie. "Ah, I must leave you to your preparations."

As he turned to go, Allie remembered the reason for his coming. "John, were you going to give me the diamonds I am to wear this evening?"

With a rueful grin, he acknowledged that that was his mission though in truth he had been seeking to steal a few moments with Allie before he had to pay homage to Lady Amabel.

Taking a velvet bag from his coat pocket, he drew out a diamond necklace and earrings. Approaching his sister-in-law, he asked, "May I?" At her nod, he placed the necklace around her neck and fastened it. Fighting off the desire to seal the clasp with a kiss, he backed away from such temptation and handed her the earrings. "You had better affix these yourself."

"Thank you, John. I will not lose them."

He smiled at her earnestness. "The only jewel I am concerned about losing is you, my dear. Take care." Without waiting for a response, he left the room.

# Chapter Eight

As the curtain lifted on the night of Allie's first visit to the theater, she stared in amazement not at the stage but at the collection of society's brightest who seemed unaware a dramatic presentation was commencing before them. Leaning over to Lord Caston who had earlier pointed out several leading lights among those gossiping in the boxes, she asked, "Why do they come here if they do not wish to see the play?"

With a rueful smile, Lord Caston admitted, "My dear Mrs. Montgomery, the object of appearing at the theater is to be seen and to see, not to watch actors. Only on rare occasions do the players on stage dominate the evening."

Allie accepted his words with a confused look and turned her own attention back to the stage, unaware that she herself was the center of interest that evening. It had not taken long for word of the identity of the slender young woman dressed in misty gray and glittering diamonds to spread through the crowds.

After various reports of her afternoon encounter in the park, everyone was determined to see for themselves the much discussed Mrs. Montgomery. Several eager souls had visited Lady Bumbry's box before the curtain rose to confirm her identity, and now many eyes were trained on her face, while she, oblivious to their stares, gave her full attention to the drama unfolding on the stage below.

\* \* \*

Lord Norwich, after dining at home with Mrs. Montgomery, called on Lady Amabel Courtney. Her ladyship had graciously accepted his flowers and apology for his relative's rash behavior.

He would have preferred escorting Mrs. Montgomery to the theater, the memory of her glowing eyes lingering in his mind. But he could best serve her by assuring Lady Amabel of his continued devotion, so he arrived there to provide escort for the evening to whatever social event the lady intended to grace.

"Well, my Lord Norwich, I wasn't sure you would care to associate with the likes of me," Lady Amabel greeted him sharply.

In what Norwich hoped was a convincing tone, he apologized. "As I stated in my note, Belle, I have no control over Mrs. Montgomery. I remain your servant, as always. Mrs. Montgomery's behavior was a reaction to your loveliness, I'm sure."

His words pleased the foolish young woman. Jealously was a reaction Lady Amabel could always understand. "Perhaps, John, but I hope you will inform her such behavior will not win her many friends in the Polite World. The ton will not stand for a merchant's daughter giving herself such airs."

"I have spoken to her, but women are capricious, Belle. As you well know."

"Won't matter soon. She'll pay for her mistakes," Sir Harold growled in the background.

"But John believes she's innocent. Is that not true, John?"

Lady Amabel's searching look caused Norwich to slant her a rueful grin. "To be truthful, Belle, I don't know anymore. Her behavior today throws a whole new light on the subject."

"Ah," the lady purred in satisfaction.

"I owe it to my brother to determine the truth," Norwich continued, "but I must admit I can see more possibilities now than ever before."

"Good. Well, it is growing late, John. Shall we attend Lady Hampton's soirée, or would you like to try a new gaming hell we discovered?"

"I don't feel so lucky this evening, Belle. Why do we not attend the party at Lady Hampton's? I would enjoy dancing with you."

Lady Amabel tapped Norwich's arm playfully with her fan. "But I do not dance, John. You must remember that I am in mourning. Even Mrs. Montgomery would find mourning a bore, I must confess, if she were allowed to move about in society. Does she complain about being left alone in the evenings?"

"No, she does not complain, Belle," Norwich responded, wondering what Lady Amabel's reaction would be when she discovered Mrs. Montgomery was enjoying the evening at the theater.

Recognizing his reluctance to discuss his sister-in-law, Amabel was gathering her cloak when her majordomo announced a surprise visitor.

One of Sir Harold and Lady Amabel's gaming cohorts, Mr. Samuels, was ushered into the room, a gleeful look on his face. Lord Norwich recognized trouble instantly.

"Belle, I knew you would want to hear right

away. Guess who is attending the theater this evening."

"I have no idea, Benny, and what makes you think I would care?"

"Mrs. Montgomery, all decked out in diamonds and the center of attention. She's with Lord Caston and Mr. Hastings."

Anger surged through Amabel. How predictable, Lord Norwich thought as he patiently waited for the storm to abate. If he wasn't so concerned about Allie, he would have found Amabel's discomfort quite amusing.

Glittering blue eyes flashed savagely as the woman struggled to bring her emotions under control. Then she turned and smiled at Norwich. "No wonder she does not complain." Her voice trembled a bit. "However, I think it is time we show Mrs. Montgomery her place is not in society."

Norwich stood expressionless.

"I have changed my mind. I do not care to attend Lady Hampton's gathering. I suddenly have a great desire to go to the theater." Her brilliant smile had a sharpness that was not lost on Norwich. "You have no objection to the theater this evening, do you, John?"

With every ounce of his being in silent revolt, he smiled and said, "A man could never object to being in the company of a Beauty such as yourself, Belle."

"Ah . . . nicely said. You could learn some pretty speeches from him, Harry."

Sir Harold did not respond to her sally, but his face reflected anger, which increased as Amabel took Norwich's arm, leaving him and Mr. Samuels to trail behind. Norwich could foresee a difficult evening. He would put nothing past her in an attempt to show the ton she had his sympathy. He hoped only that Mrs. Montgomery would understand.

The first intermission had almost ended and Mrs. Montgomery had met so many gentlemen she found it impossible to remember half the names. As the crowd in the box lessened, she enjoyed a few moments chatting with Lady Bumbry, an older and very sensible woman.

As they talked, Allie suddenly broke off in mid-sentence. Over Lady Bumbry's shoulder, she watched in growing consternation as Lady Amabel Courtney and her three escorts made their entrance into a box almost opposite their own.

"My dear, whatever is the matter? You have gone very pale," Lady Bumbry asked in concern.

Brought back to reality, Mrs. Montgomery was making her apologies when Lord Caston stepped forward to the two ladies. "Take no notice, madam."

"Take no notice of what, Giles? What is happening?" the older woman asked in confusion.

Lord Caston hastened to whisper discreetly to Lady Bumbry, warning of the newest arrivals before turning to Mrs. Montgomery and engaging her in a conversation that he hoped would distract her. Allie struggled to concentrate on what he was saying, but all she could see was the enemy.

The woman's dress was outrageous. It hardly

mattered whether it was black or brilliant red, as its bodice was almost nonexistent and the material so thin it hid little of her charms. The way she clung to Lord Norwich and pressed her body against his at the slightest provocation, Allie knew, were tricks of a demimondaine. Her cheeks flamed as she tried to ignore such blatant behavior, but her efforts were fruitless. Lord Caston was greatly relieved when the curtain rose on the second act. And he planned a few words he intended to share with his dear friend Norwich before this night was over.

Mr. Browning, unaware of the dramatic events of the evening, arrived at Lord Norwich's town house with a few tidbits of information and an eagerness to discover if the others had made any progress. Time was running out and he was becoming concerned at their lack of success.

After being admitted by Jeffers, he discovered that both Lord Norwich and Mrs. Montgomery were out for the evening, and he seized the opportunity to visit another member of the household.

"Would you ask Miss Thompson if she would see me for a few minutes?" he asked pleasantly.

Jeffers stiffened imperceptively. "Of course, Mr. Browning. Would you care to wait in the morning room?"

"I think I would prefer the library, if that is satisfactory, Jeffers. I do not believe Lord Norwich would mind."

Jeffers himself could think of no objection to this plan, so he escorted Mr. Browning to his master's library after dispatching a footman to search out Mavis.

As the butler was about to close the door on Mr. Browning, the man of business thought of something else. "Oh, Jeffers, would you serve tea? I find myself in need of sustenance, and I'm sure Miss Thompson would enjoy it also."

"Of course, sir," the butler stoically agreed, but Mr. Browning studied him carefully as he withdrew. Jeffers had never before shown any disinclination to serve him with or without his master, and during Lord Norwich's absences, he had had several visits to the house. Was there a problem of which he was not aware? He pondered the situation while awaiting Mavis. So deep in thought was he, he was unaware of the slender figure who slipped into the library to stand silently awaiting his attention.

Turning back from the window, Mr. Browning was surprised to find Mavis. "I did not hear you enter. Why did you not call my attention?"

The young woman kept her head down and swiftly executed a graceful curtsy. Mr. Browning, in the act of reaching for her hand, stared at her intently. First Jeffers and now Mavis. He wondered if there was a connection.

"Mavis?" When the young woman made no comment, he drew closer and raised her face up with his hand. Reddened eyes told their own tale. Mr. Browning drew Mavis over to the sofa before he questioned the cause of her tears.

"What is wrong? What has happened to overset you?" he asked gently.

"Nothing, sir," Mavis responded quietly, with only a tremor in her voice.

"Mavis, this is not like you. Has something happened to Mrs. Montgomery?"

"No, sir."

"Lord Norwich?"

"Not that I know of, sir."

"Then it must be something personal. Is it . . . is it because of our last meeting?" A quick shake of her head led him to ask, "Has it anything to do with Jeffers . . . or any of the other servants?"

He caught a glimpse of big blue eyes flashing before they hid beneath golden lashes.

"Aha! You see, I am becoming quite good at discovering puzzles. When I arrived, I found a stiffness in Jeffers that I had never noticed before. While I might have offended him in some way, I did not think it. Therefore, I determined it must be something about the staff. And now you turn up with red eyes and will not talk to me."

When there was no response from his companion, Mr. Browning decided to use a slightly more underhanded approach. "Of course, since I am the recipient of both cases of antipathy, perhaps it is me. Have I offended you in some way, Mavis? I vow I never intended to . . ."

"Oh, no, sir! How could you think so, when you rescued me from that p-place."

"Ah, then we are friends?"

"I . . . I will be forever in your debt, sir."

"That is not what I asked. Are we not friends, Mavis?"

"I . . . I . . . we cannot be friends, but I

would do anything for you," Mavis said, as tears rolled reluctantly down her cheeks.

"Why can we not be friends?"

"Because I . . . I am a servant, Mr. Browning."

"The other servants are giving you a hard time?"

"I never . . . please, Mr. Browning, I never said that! You mustn't . . ."

"Calm down, Mavis. What we discuss here this evening is only between the two of us, as friends. I would never betray your confidence, as I know you would never betray mine."

His faith in her freed more tears and Mavis covered her face with shaking hands. "I . . . thank you, sir. I wouldn't ever . . . ever do anything to hurt you."

"And that is something for which I am very grateful. But would you do something to help me?"

Mavis's eyes flew to his face again. "Of course, Mr. Browning. Anything! What can I do to help you?"

"Nothing at the moment, Mavis, but why, if we are friends, do I not have the same privilege? Why can I not help you?"

"That's not fair!" Mavis protested, annoyed with Mr. Browning's neat trap.

"Come, Mavis, enough. Tell me what is troubling you."

"No."

"The staff is jealous of your special privileges and are being unkind to you."

"No! That is . . . not unkind . . . just not

friendly. They don't like being made to wait on me when I am also a . . . a servant."

"Only unfriendly? Not cruel? Because Lord Norwich would never tolerate . . ."

"No, I promise, Mr. Browning. It is just that I get a little lonely . . . and I'm worried about Mrs. Montgomery . . . and . . . and about me."

Mr. Browning subdued the strong urge he felt to take the woeful figure in his arms and offer comfort. He sought for a more acceptable way to express reassurance.

"We will find a way to save Mrs. Montgomery, Mavis, I promise you. And . . . and if we are unable to prove her innocence . . . well, you must promise not to reveal this to either of the others but . . . I have been thinking perhaps we could assist Mrs. Montgomery to leave the country. Either for the Continent or perhaps even America."

For the first time that evening he saw the Mavis who had protected Mrs. Montgomery for two months in Newgate. Eagerly she leaned toward him. "Do you think it possible? Could we help her escape?"

"I believe we could, Mavis."

"And I could go with her, to protect her."

"Would you mind leaving England, Mavis?"

"Oh, no, Mr. Browning. I was thinking, if . . . if something happened to Mrs. Montgomery, I would leave anyway. I am learning how to read and write. She's teaching me. And when she's not here, I work hard learning everything I can, so I can become an indentured servant."

"An indentured servant? Perhaps Lord Norwich would . . ."

"No! Lord Norwich doesn't owe me anything. I can pay my own way," she stated firmly before looking at her companion. "Is it that you think no one would want to hire me?"

Mr. Browning, recognizing the seriousness of her question, studied his companion closely. Since her ordeal in the prison, she had lost her starved look and her complexion had taken on a creamy color, emphasizing her large blue eyes. Her hair, clean and neatly plaited, resembled a golden halo around her head.

Her gray servant's dress was appropriate and tidy, but it did not hide the attractions of her body, more apparent to Mr. Browning than ever before. He understood the problem Mavis had had and would be likely to have again with unscrupulous employers.

"How old are you, Mavis?" Mr. Browning asked abruptly.

"I . . . I'm almost nineteen. Is something wrong? Am I too young?"

"I am sure you would have no difficulty finding someone willing to take you on as an indentured servant, Mavis, but . . . you are much too young to face the world on your own."

"But, Mr. Browning, I've been on my own since my parents died. And I would have managed just fine if Mrs. Dalrymple had not lied."

"But don't you see, Mavis, the reason she lied was because you are a very attractive young woman with no one to protect you." He ignored her flushed cheeks and downcast eyes and continued, "You see, that is the problem with your becoming an indentured servant. What if . . . your employer decided he wanted . . . demanded . . ."

"I'd kill him!"

"And then you would be put back in prison and I would not be there to rescue you."

Mavis slumped down into the sofa. "Sometimes I think it might be easier to just give up and end it all."

This time Mr. Browning did not refrain from taking the young woman into his arms, holding her tightly against him. "No, Mavis! And I do not want to hear you talk so again. We will find a way. You must believe me." He released her slightly to look into her face. "You must promise me you will let me help you, that you will not take such a cowardly way out."

Mavis, finding comfort in the protective, warm embrace, was reluctant to move from Mr. Browning's hold, but she nodded hesitantly and pulled away.

There was an awkward pause as each secretly savored the pleasure of their embrace. Mavis broke the silence eventually with a question that brought Mr. Browning back to the original purpose of his call.

"Did you come to see Lord Norwich?"

"Oh . . . yes, I discovered some minor items I thought I might discuss with him."

"News about Mrs. Montgomery?"

"In a roundabout way. Several of Mr. Montgomery's other sporting friends are in debt, but that was not unexpected. And Sir Harold has had particularly heavy gaming debts recently that he has not been able to meet. I expected debts, but these are excessive."

"That makes it even more likely he murdered Mr. Montgomery for his money."

"Yes, but that was already fairly well established, at least to the four of us. I've been checking to discover who the best forgers are. It would help if we could find the author of that will. The other piece of information was more interesting, I believe. Sir Harold's valet, a man called Ogden, was in prison serving a life term when Sir Harold paid the nominal fee to have him released for thievery and hired him as his valet."

"But, Mr. Browning, innocent people get put in prison. I certainly know that."

"You are correct, Mavis, and normally I try to give people the benefit of the doubt, but Sir Harold dismissed the valet who had served him for a number of years and hired this man only a fortnight before Mr. Montgomery's murder."

"You think he found this Ogden to do his dirty work for him?"

"It looks that way to me. Sir Harold was once a decent sort who fell into the trap of many a green youth. He lost everything to the cards and has had to live by his wits. But I never thought him a murderer. I'm sure he hired his new valet for that purpose, but I have no proof."

"No . . . and proof is what we need."

They both sat silently contemplating the situation before Mr. Browning returned to their earlier situation.

"Mavis, if you feel you cannot remain here for

any reason, I want to give you the address of my home. You can always come there."

Surprising a strange look in her eyes, Mr. Browning's cheeks flushed as he hurriedly assured her, "I live with my parents. My mother is always home. We would be happy to give you a place to stay until we determine your future."

He took out his business card and handed it to her. He had a growing fear that Mavis might one day disappear with no one to assist her or to protect her. "Promise me you will do nothing without consulting me!"

His concern was heartwarming, and Mavis could do nothing but promise, though she wondered if the day might come when she felt compelled to break that promise.

Their tête-à-tête was disrupted by the sound of approaching voices. Mr. Browning and Mavis rose from the sofa to face the door as it opened.

Those entering seemed unaware of the room's occupants as their argument continued.

"But couldn't you have escorted that harpy . . . that woman to another social event?"

"I had every intention in the world of doing so, Caston, but once she discovered Mrs. Montgomery was attending the theater, she determined she too must make an appearance."

"But why did you tell her?"

"I didn't . . ." Lord Norwich began in a frustrated roar when his eyes fell upon the other two. "Browning! Mavis! I beg your pardon. I did not realize . . . Caston, Billy, I believe you have made the acquaintance of Mr. Browning, my man of business, and this is . . . this is Miss Thompson, Mrs. Montgomery's companion. These are two of my friends, Lord Caston and Mr. Hastings."

Mrs. Montgomery moved forward to clasp hands with Mavis and draw her down to the sofa while the gentlemen found suitable resting places around them. At that moment, Jeffers entered the library with the earlier requested tea, unaware of the new arrivals, who had been let in by one of the underfootmen.

"Lord Norwich! I was unaware of your return, my lord. Mr. Browning requested tea. Shall I . . ."

"Yes, bring some more cups, though we gentlemen may choose something a little stronger. This evening calls for it."

The butler and his retinue deposited their trays and withdrew only to return shortly with additions to the tea tray. While waiting, Mrs. Montgomery distributed the offerings, though she herself had absolutely no stomach for the delicacies before her.

Once the servants had finally withdrawn, Lord Caston returned to the attack.

"But if you did not tell her, how could she possibly have known Mrs. Montgomery was at the theater?"

"Very simply. A Mr. Benjamin Samuels, after catching sight of Mrs. Montgomery in Lady Bumbry's box, rushed from the theater to share the information with the one person he felt sure would be interested. We were just about to leave. Another five minutes and we would have missed him," Lord Norwich explained with disgust.

"Samuels, bad ton," Billy assured everyone. "Lady Amabel's behavior was bad, too. And her dress . . ."

"Left nothing to the imagination," Lord Norwich assured him bluntly. "I am aware of that, Billy, but I was unable to protest. She was waiting to see if I would back down after our encounter in the park. I had no choice."

"You needn't have looked like you enjoyed it," Allie muttered under her breath, her jealousy overcoming her discretion. Her hands flew up to cover her mouth when she realized she had spoken the words aloud.

"I assure you, madam, I found no enjoyment in my evening at all. I only sat through it for your benefit, and if you wish for me to cease my efforts on your behalf, you have only to inform me."

The icicles that filled the air after Lord Norwich's speech were apparent to everyone in the library. Allie's cheeks flamed and her apology was stiff with embarrassment. "I appreciate your efforts on my behalf, Lord Norwich. Please forgive me."

Lord Caston broke the awkward silence. "Well, now that we all know what happened could not be avoided, what is next?"

No one had any immediate suggestions. Finally, Mr. Browning offered, "I discovered a few tidbits of information today, one of which might be interesting."

As he revealed his information about Sir Harold's valet, Mavis caught Allie's hand in hers and gave it a gentle squeeze. Clearly it had been a difficult evening for her friend.

"Perhaps that is the man I saw at my brother's house. That would link Sir Harold to the second murder. I'll have my groom see if he can recognize him while we . . . I don't know what we can do. Any suggestions?"

After a lengthy silence, Mavis began timidly, "My lord?"

"Yes, Mavis?"

"Have you . . . I mean, might you not hint to Lady Amabel that you would like to marry her if the murder was cleared up? Maybe she will betray Sir Harold if she sees a bigger catch."

"You would never propose marriage to her!" Allie protested, her heart in her throat.

"Mavis said hint, not propose. But I would even do that if it meant I could free you," Lord Norwich assured her angrily.

"Perhaps it would be more effective if I flirted with Sir Harold. He might expose Lady Amabel if he thought I had an interest in him!"

"That is an absurd idea, and I completely forbid your doing any such thing!" Lord Norwich roared. "You are under my protection. I will not have you even speaking to that man! Do you hear me, Allie?"

Lord Caston smiled ruefully at the table-turning. "I am sure she hears you quite well, Norwich, as well as everyone else in the house and perhaps a few streets over as well. I'm quite certain Mrs. Montgomery was speaking from frustration and has no serious intentions toward Sir Harold."

"No, of course not. I . . . am sorry, my lord. I . . . I believe it is time I retired. I am very tired," Allie said as she rose. "I . . . I thank you for your efforts on my behalf, gentlemen. I—I am sorry things have not turned out as well as they might have," she finished tearfully before departing, accompanied by her friend.

Lord Norwich actually started in her direction, his desire to reassure her overcoming all rules of accepted behavior, but he was stopped by the closing door. Ducking his head, he turned back to the fireplace, hoping the others had not noticed his behavior.

"Women," Billy said mournfully. "Can't hold a conversation without tears. My sister always used to get her way with m'father. Just cry a few tears, and he'd give in."

The other three nodded in agreement with Lord Norwich's tightly voiced response, "I know exactly how he felt."

## Chapter Nine

"I made a fool of myself, didn't I?" Allie burst out as Mavis silently helped her undress.

"No . . . you just . . ."

"Showed my jealousy of that creature!" Allie fumed as Mavis continued to release the tiny buttons that ran down the back of the dress. "You should have seen her, Mavis! She draped herself all over Lord Norwich the entire evening. And her dress! It was cut so low, it is a wonder she did not lose it entirely!"

"She sounds a rare bird. But I'm sure Lord Norwich cares nothing for her."

"You may be right, but he gave no indication of such this evening. I could scarcely bear to watch him catering to that woman!" She paled as she realized what she had said. "I must not . . . I cannot allow myself to feel . . . to love his lordship," she whispered.

"Why not?" Mavis asked bluntly.

"Because I am not an aristocrat. The only reason Mr. Montgomery married me was for my money. Lord Norwich has a large fortune of his own. He can choose from among the most beautiful of the debutantes."

"But you are beautiful. This evening, in your new gown, with diamonds, I bet there was no one prettier there."

Allie gave a watery chuckle. "Thank you, Mavis, but I fear you are wrong. My, I have never seen such beautiful gowns and jewels."

"Well, I still think Lord Norwich cares for you," Mavis stubbornly insisted.

"Only because he is responsible for me. Once I am freed from the possibility of hanging, he will have nothing more to do with me."

"He will not do that. He will always . . . care for you, even if it is not all that you want."

"I know," Allie admitted with a sigh. "And I must put aside such silliness and discover a plan.

I think I should go out more into society. I think Lady Amabel was most disturbed that I appeared this evening."

"I am sure you are right. She cannot spread lies about your quality when others have discovered you are a lady."

"Yes. The difficulty will be convincing Lord Norwich. He was not happy about my going to the theater, though he agreed because his friends insisted."

The two women spent almost an hour devising various schemes for convincing Norwich of the value of Allie's appearance in society. Some of Allie's ideas were so preposterous, both women laughed, but there was also a seriousness to their plotting.

Finally, Allie, exhausted by the evening's events, rose to prepare for bed. "Mavis," she said suddenly, "if Lord Norwich does not . . . care for me as I do him, I will not be able to remain here, no matter how kind he may be."

"I know."

"We will be fine," Allie assured her friend with a trembling voice. "I have plenty of money to support us, but . . . it would be so hard to not see him."

"Yes," Mavis agreed fervently, another face in her thoughts.

"Oh, Mavis . . ." Allie began as tears rolled down her face, "what am I going to do?"

Putting her arms around her friend, Mavis patted her soothingly on her back. "I don't know. I just don't know."

\*   \*   \*

Having switched from tea to a more potent drink, the gentlemen settled themselves around the fire, their faces reflecting frustration and despair.

Lord Caston finally roused himself to observe, "Your information about Sir Harold's valet sounds promising, Mr. Browning. How did you come across it?"

"One of my clerks, in assisting one of my other clients, came across the information in a court record and brought it to my attention, since he knew I had an interest in Sir Harold."

After a round of encouraging comments, another silence followed. Finally, Mr. Browning asked, "What else can be done, my lord? Do you still expect difficulties from Lady Norwich?"

"Nasty lady," Mr. Hastings commented.

"I forgot to inform you, Mr. Browning. I think someone has already made an attempt on Mrs. Montgomery's life." He told him about the appearance of the deadly asp in the dressmaker's box.

"But the ladies were not harmed?" Mr. Browning asked with great concern.

Lord Norwich studied his man of business, gauging his interest in Mrs. Montgomery. He considered it to be excessive, considering the man had just seen her. "Of course she was not harmed. I know how to care for my guests, Mr. Browning."

The reproof in his voice surprised his listeners. Mr. Browning knew he had offended, though he did not understand how. He arose immediately, prepared to depart.

"Excuse me, my lord. It is late. I will let you know if I discover any additional information."

"Sit down, man. I did not mean to dismiss you."

"Nor did I mean to cast doubts on your abilities, my lord," Mr. Browning said as he lowered himself back into his chair. "My concern was whether Mrs. Montgomery or . . . anyone else . . . might have been frightened."

"Mrs. Montgomery is safe. Actually, it was Mr. Hastings who discovered the viper. And I will confess that I almost did not check the delivery due to my impatience. So you would have been justified in casting aspersions on my diligence. However, I promise it will not happen again. I will give Mrs. Montgomery strict instructions about leaving the house, and may I assume, gentlemen, if I am not available, one of you will respond to any request for an escort?"

At their agreement, he continued. "The servants here are to be trusted, but I would feel more at ease if our staff were increased, preferably with tall, muscular men. Is it possible for you to handle that, Mr. Browning? Everyone must be carefully screened. Perhaps even a couple of Bow Street Runners might be a good idea. Could we hire some who could act as footmen?"

"I doubt they would reach Jeffers's high standards, but they would suffice."

"Good. And if we can determine whether Sir Harold's valet is the servant seen at Edward's house, we can have him detained. That should

sufficiently disturb Sir Harold to make him care-
less at the very least." Lord Norwich paused and
sighed. "And I suppose I must continue my pursuit of Lady Amabel."

Lord Caston grinned. "A difficult task, Norwich, and you have all our sympathies."

"You laugh, Caston, but I can assure you it is a
despicable job. The woman is self-centered and
vile when you consider how she has treated Allie,
I mean Mrs. Montgomery."

"Bad ton, too. You will have no reputation to
speak of when this is over," Billy assured him.

"After this evening, I surely have very little
left, anyway. The woman behaved like a light-
skirt!"

"Well, you must console yourself with the
thought of the envy you aroused in the hearts of
the young bucks," Lord Caston advised, enjoying
his friend's discomfort.

"It is easy for you to say so, knowing you will
be escorting Mrs. Montgomery."

"Mrs. Montgomery is a true lady," Billy pro-
nounced. "Proud to escort her. Take her for a ride
in the park tomorrow. Tell her to wear lilac. A
nice set of amethysts, too. Do you have them?"

"Billy, I refuse to discuss Mrs. Montgomery's
wardrobe. You will just have to trust to her judgment."

"Come, Billy," Lord Caston said, rising, "I believe we have overstayed our welcome. You can
trust Mrs. Montgomery's dress sense." Turning to
Norwich, he added, "You can assure Mrs. Montgomery of our willingness to wait upon her
whenever she needs an escort. And, of course,

whatever we can do to help will be our pleasure, Norwich."

"Thanks, Caston, Billy," Lord Norwich said as he escorted his friends to the door, motioning to Mr. Browning, behind his back, to remain a few moments.

When he returned to the room, Mr. Browning was waiting expectantly. Lord Norwich paced across the room, a frown on his face. Mr. Browning grew concerned. There must be something seriously wrong, so much so that Lord Norwich did not want to discuss it before his friends. Mr. Browning's anxiety grew with each step of his host.

Finally, Lord Norwich sat down across from Mr. Browning. "I want to ask your intentions toward Mrs. Montgomery."

Mr. Browning, prepared to learn about some new attempt on Mrs. Montgomery's life, stared at Lord Norwich. "I . . . I beg your pardon, my lord?"

"You heard me, man! I want to know your intentions toward Mrs. Montgomery."

"Well, I . . . I intend to serve her in whatever way possible. Certainly I will willingly continue as her man of business and . . . and I will assist you in clearing her name . . ." His voice trailed off as he watched the frustration visible on Lord Norwich's face. There was something here he did not understand.

"I mean your . . . your romantic intentions!" Norwich snapped.

Dumbfounded, Mr. Browning stared at his employer. When it became evident to Norwich the man had no response, he said, "Well, you have certainly worked intensely on her behalf, and . . . and you have expressed considerable concern. It appeared to me . . . damn it, man, say something!"

"Certainly, my lord, but . . . but anyone would have been concerned, given the circumstances. I . . . I certainly admire Mrs. Montgomery for her fortitude and bravery in trying circumstances. And my sense of justice is outraged at what has happened to her, but I swear I never . . . it never occurred to me . . . I do not think Mrs. Montgomery . . ."

"I did not mean to infer Mrs. Montgomery felt . . . felt anything toward you other than gratitude. I just thought . . . damn! It appears I misread the situation. I apologize."

"No apologies are necessary, my lord. Mrs. Montgomery is a wonderful woman but . . . but she is above my touch."

"Such a marriage would not be unheard of, Browning."

"Lord Norwich, I have great admiration for Mrs. Montgomery, but I have been a bachelor for all my forty years."

"She will be a rich prize once her name is cleared," the Earl persisted.

"But I am not a fortune hunter, my lord."

"I did not mean . . . damn it, I am apologizing more this evening than I ever have in my entire life. But I sensed something. I know it! This evening there was something . . ."

Mr. Browning rose from his chair, his cheeks slightly flushed, and he walked to the mantel, his back to his inquisitor. Lord Norwich waited, disquieted by the man's reaction.

Mr. Browning turned back to face the Earl, a strange look on his face. "You are correct, my lord," he began, holding up a hand when his host would have interrupted him. "But there is an error in the identity of the object of my interest."

He moved from the mantel and began pacing in front of the fireplace. "I have not admitted it even to myself until this evening, but . . . I feel a strong attraction for . . . for Mavis . . . Miss Thompson." He glanced warily at Norwich, as if he expected laughter or contempt, but when there was no response, only intense interest, he continued. "She is a remarkable young woman. And she is quite beautiful, with her golden hair, her figure, her . . ."

"I have no argument with what you have said, Browning, and it is none of my business what you choose to do, but . . . in spite of all that, your parents, your position . . . the girl is a servant!"

Mr. Browning halted his pacing, his eyes staring into the distance, as he responded. "Miss Thompson is capable of becoming many things. But you are correct, my lord, there could be difficulties. I had not admitted my attraction until this evening. When we talked alone . . . and she needed comforting, it was most difficult to refrain from taking her home at once. Not that she would go. Her loyalty to Mrs. Montgomery is remarkable."

"Perhaps for the sake of your family and career, you should consider an arrangement other than marriage," Norwich suggested.

Mr. Browning was aware that mistresses were the norm rather than the exception in society. But the thought of betraying Mavis in such a way appalled him.

"No, my lord," he stated firmly, "whatever I decide about Miss Thompson, it will not be to . . . to betray her in that manner."

Norwich's respect for Browning had increased since his return. He accepted his reply without protestation, though he felt the man might be making a mistake. To marry beneath him socially could cause great difficulties.

He had seen too many examples of it among his peers. And he had suffered from its effects in his own family when his father had married his stepmother. Her family was considerably inferior to his. The result of their union had not been a happy one, either, particularly to him.

"My lord . . . pardon my curiosity, but it concerns Miss Thompson and therefore . . . possibly myself. What is to happen to Mrs. Montgomery?"

"Why, we are trying . . . going to prove her innocent."

"Yes, my lord, but, assuming we do, what will happen to her then?"

"She will do whatever she pleases. Perhaps travel, or retire to the country."

"But not life among the ton?"

"If she wants to live here in London, there is no difficulty. I will certainly aid her in whatever she chooses."

"I do not mean to pry, but I fear Miss Thompson would refuse to leave Mrs. Montgomery if she is left alone."

"Of course she will not be alone. I will be here. We are family . . ." Lord Norwich paced across the room. "Damn," he muttered quietly. "I might as well admit it, Browning. I kept you here to question your intentions toward Mrs. Montgomery because I was jealous! I . . . I do not know . . . I am not sure how she feels . . . but I can assure you she will be protected."

Mr. Browning smiled warmly. "I am pleased that you, ah, appreciate Mrs. Montgomery, Lord Norwich. I, too, have not put it to the touch with Miss Thompson. I thought it best to wait until Mrs. Montgomery's problem is solved." He moved to the decanter and refilled their glasses. "If I may, my lord, a toast to our ladies."

Lord Norwich joined him, raising his glass. "To the ladies, Browning. May they be freed from this damned mess, and may their hearts be generous to us."

The two men drank and then smiled sheepishly, unnerved by their conversation. Lord Norwich added hastily, "You do understand that none of this must be spoken about outside these four walls, Browning."

"Of course, my lord. And now, I must return home, if you will excuse me."

Lord Norwich remained in the library, his dark head bent, his blue eyes watching the flames lick the logs. Tonight was the first time he had vocalized the thoughts that had been growing ever since he first met Allie. They had grown so strong, they could no longer be denied, and yet he must keep his hopes to himself until he could ensure her freedom. Then, and only then, could he lay his heart at her feet.

## Chapter Ten

When Allie dressed the next morning, she spent considerable time choosing from her rapidly expanding wardrobe. She needed the confidence her newfound elegance could give her. Her first thought had been to remain in her room, hidden from Lord Norwich's eyes. But that was a cowardly act, and even embarrassment could not be worse than what she had already survived.

Besides, she argued with herself as Mavis buttoned up the back of a pink morning dress that brought a bloom to her cheeks (she saw no need to don mourning in the privacy of Lord Norwich's home), she may have demonstrated her jealousy of Lady Amabel, but Lord Norwich might not have realized it stemmed from a strong attachment to himself.

Allie stirred restively at the thought. She had vowed to not think of John in that manner until her future was determined, but she found it almost impossible to keep the promise. He dominated her mind whatever task she had before her, and she feared she might slip and expose her true feelings. That thought spurred her to concentrate on other things.

She squared her shoulders, as if bracing for battle, determined to find a way to clear herself and make a new life.

"Stop your squirming, or I'll never get finished," Mavis admonished.

"Sorry, Mavis," Allie said, gazing at her abigail in the looking glass. "Mavis, I wish you would wear something besides that awful gray. It is so depressing."

The girl sighed, looking down at her plain dress. "It's fitting for a servant."

"But I didn't intend for you to be a servant. Why can you not just be my friend, my companion?"

"Because I'm a servant and always will be. Things don't change just because you want them to."

"Are the servants making your life difficult?" Allie demanded, her eyes searching her friend's face.

"No, not difficult . . . they—they're not too friendly, but . . ."

Allie turned around in spite of Mavis's work. "After I am cleared of the charges, Mavis, I promise things will be better. We will move someplace different, away from London, to our very own house, and you shall not be a servant. I have been thinking about the Lake District. I have always wanted to see it. We would . . . we could be happy there, couldn't we?" She shut away the pain she experienced at even thinking of never seeing Lord Norwich again.

Mavis shook her head sadly. "No, wherever you are in England, other folks will have nothing to do with you if you try to pass me off as quality."

"Mavis, with the right clothes and a little more practice with your speech, you would be as acceptable as anyone." She already considered Mavis to be more of a lady than Lady Amabel.

"We'll see, love . . . we'll see. Now turn around and let me finish doing you up. And no squirming, now." Mavis kept her plans of traveling to America to herself. Time enough for that when her friend was happy and settled. But Mavis had heard about America enough to know that a woman had a chance to be something other than what she had been born to, and she wanted that opportunity.

After sitting alone over one of Cook's superb breakfasts, Allie retired to the morning room. It was well proportioned, done up in several shades of blue, with touches of yellow that always made Allie think of the sun peeping through clouds after a spring shower. There she picked up a piece of stitchery she had begun only the day before, unconsciously returning to the strict training of her childhood to relieve her troubled mind.

Things seemed to be happening quickly, but not quickly enough to resolve all of her problems. She reminded herself of the deadline she faced. Only three more weeks before she was to be tried for a crime she didn't commit. A shiver passed over her slender body as she pictured that feared day's events.

"Madam." Jeffers's voice interrupted her.

"Ah! Oh, Jeffers, you startled me! What is it?"

"You have a caller . . . Lady Jersey."

Even had Mrs. Montgomery not recognized the name of one of society's most influential ladies, reverently discussed in the hinterlands and much feared among the ton, Jeffers's tone of voice would have alerted her to the importance of her guest. Even in her remote village, Allie had heard her aunt and her crony discuss Lady Jersey and the Fashionable World she ruled. "Lady Jersey? Here? She must have come to see Lord Norwich."

"No, madam. She asked if you were at home."

"Why . . . why, of course I am at home. Please show her in." As the butler turned to follow her bidding, she added, "Jeffers . . . do I look presentable?"

The butler gave no hint of the fatherly feelings the young lady's anxious face evoked in him but answered gravely, "You look a fair treat, madam."

As she awaited Lady Jersey, Allie picked up her stitchery in a desperate attempt to calm her anxious nerves. What could Lady Jersey want with her? Perhaps she had come to reprimand her for snubbing Lady Amabel. Perhaps she considered it highly improper for an accused murderess to appear in society at all. And what if . . .

"Lady Jersey," Jeffers intoned, holding the door wide for her ladyship, wrapped in a rich purple walking dress trimmed in sable. Allie rose from the sofa to meet her unexpected guest. "Lady Jersey, please, won't you be seated."

"Thank you, Mrs. Montgomery. I hope you will forgive this intrusion," the lady said with all the confidence of one who knows her every visit is cause for celebration. "I was eager to meet Society's latest heroine."

"Heroine? I don't know what you are . . . to whom you are referring. I have done nothing to deserve such praise."

"Oh?" Lady Jersey smilingly drawled. "Are you not the young lady who slew a particular Medusa in the park yesterday?"

Comprehension flooded Allie and her cheeks were red as she sought to dismiss her actions. "Really, Lady Jersey, I did nothing! I only . . . it was . . . I didn't know how to . . ."

"Do not dare apologize, young lady. You have accomplished something many a dowager with a marriageable daughter would have given her life to do. And with such cool self-possession. You have caused a stir among a much-sated crowd. I vow I wish I had been able to do as much!"

"Thank you, my lady."

"And then to appear last night, cool as can be, in the company of two of the most eligible bachelors in the kingdom, was a piece of such courage as I have yet to see. You have my admiration, Mrs. Montgomery."

"Oh, please, my lady, you exaggerate."

"Perhaps," Lady Jersey agreed with a winsome smile. "But I did not come to praise your behavior, as much as I admire it. I want you to attend my ball tomorrow night." As Allie began to protest such an honor, Lady Jersey continued. "I know it is short notice, but I am determined to have the coup of the season. You cannot imagine how many members of Society are eager to meet you. I have always set the fashion, and I refuse to lag behind now. You must come."

"But, Lady Jersey, I have not . . ."

"Sally, how nice to see you again."

Both ladies were startled by Lord Norwich's arrival, and neither was fooled by his expression of pleasure. The austerity of his dark features belied his words.

Lady Jersey extended her hand to be saluted and drew her gallant host down beside her on the gilded sofa. "Just the gentleman I need. I have been trying to convince your charming sister-in-law that she should attend my ball tomorrow evening. It is to be the hit of the season," she added with no modesty but great accuracy, "and I am determined to have her there. It will ensure my party's success."

"You need no insurance, Sally. All of the ton have been clamoring for an invitation for weeks."

"Humor me, dear boy. Tell me you will escort Mrs. Montgomery tomorrow evening."

"Sally, I fear you must hold me excused. I have already made another commitment and I must not break it."

Allie guessed with whom her brother-in-law would be enjoying his evening and frantically sought to control the jealousy that rose within her.

"Hmmm." Lady Jersey studied him for a moment. "Never fear, I intend to extend an invitation to her as well. But I fear that eliminates you as an escort to Mrs. Montgomery. I will ask either Lord Caston or Mr. Hastings to accompany you, Mrs. Montgomery. I am sure either will be overjoyed to do so. They both seemed content in your company last evening."

"Sally, what are you up to?"

"Tut, tut. Never question my intentions, dear boy. You might not like the answer."

"I will not have you using my sister-in-law to further your own amusements!"

Both ladies watched their companion as he jumped to his feet and strode across the room. Turning around, he encountered Allie's questioning gaze. "Do you not understand?" he demanded impatiently. "She is planning a confrontation between you and Lady Amabel to provide entertainment at her ball."

Allie, as comprehension dawned, turned to stare at Lady Jersey.

"Do not think me so terrible, my dear," Lady Jersey pleaded lightly. "True, it would enliven my evening to see the two of you meet, but I mean you no harm. You have proven yourself a worthy adversary for the likes of her."

"Sally! You don't understand the seriousness of the situation. We are not talking about social reputation. We are talking about Mrs. Montgomery's life!"

Lady Jersey's eyebrows rose as she questioned, "Life? Are you saying Lady Amabel will try to kill Mrs. Montgomery? Come now, John, surely you jest."

"No, I am not jesting, and no, I will not say anything more. I have said too much already."

"John." Allie's soft voice interrupted the exchange. "I think attending Lady Jersey's ball is not such a bad idea. I had already determined that I should appear in Society more."

"Allie, please, I know what is best . . ."

"Why, Mrs. Montgomery?" Lady Jersey questioned curiously, ignoring Norwich.

"It is necessary for Lady Amabel to be shaken from her plan as well as a . . . companion of hers. A public confrontation might accomplish that sooner than any private persuasions." Though her words were directed at Lady Jersey, Allie pinned her eyes on her brother-in-law.

"Allie! I will not allow—"

"I have always found public encounters to be most effective, my dear, and I would love to assist you. Lady Amabel is not a favorite of mine . . . nor of anyone else with whom I associate."

"I cannot tell you more, Lady Jersey," Allie confided, aware of the woman's reputation as a gossip, "but I will certainly attend your ball. Oh, and could I ask you to invite Sir Harold Baynham also?" At Lady Jersey's look of distaste, she hastily added, "I know he is not . . . *comme il faut*, but he is completely necessary to my plan."

"Then, of course, he will be invited. But for a price. I must be the first in the Polite World to know the whole story."

"I promise, and your assistance will be rewarded if things come out right. If not . . . then I will instruct Lord Norwich to inform you after . . . after my demise."

Lady Jersey glanced sharply from Allie's down-cast head to Norwich's stern visage. "Then the rumor is true: You did murder your husband?"

Allie's head came up, her chin firming as she answered quietly, "No, my lady. But unless my husband's true killer can be discovered within three weeks, I will hang."

For once in her life, Lady Jersey had nothing to say. Recognizing her discomfort, Allie sought to allay it. "Never fear, Lady Jersey, I shall not go quietly to the gallows. I intend to discover the true villain, and your invitation will assist me."

"Then I am delighted to be of service. You have surprised me, Mrs. Montgomery. I came here expecting a graceless hayseed. I shall leave happy to have made the acquaintance of a true aristocrat."

Allie blushed, her cheeks matching the color of her gown. "Thank you, my lady. That is a very fine compliment."

Embarrassed at her unusual solemnity, Lady Jersey stood. "Well, I shall look forward to your arrival tomorrow evening. And I shall return home and write out an invitation to that creature and her escort. I cannot bear the thought of delivering it in person, but I will be sure it arrives and let you know when it is accepted."

"Thank you, Lady Jersey. You are kindness itself," Allie said as she rose to stand beside her guest.

"It is gracious of you to say so when I had nothing but my own amusement in mind when I arrived, child."

"It is how you leave that is important, my lady,

not how you arrive. And you leave with my gratitude."

Lady Jersey studied the young woman before she turned to the man. "This is the only wise choice your brother ever made, and he was too much of a fool to realize it." Without another word, she left the room, leaving two silent figures behind her.

Allie sat down abruptly on the blue sofa, her shaky limbs no longer willing to hold her upright. At the movement, Norwich whirled around to stare at her accusingly. "How could you agree to such a plan? You could be killed! I'm trying to save your life."

"Please, John . . . I truly do have a plan . . . I think."

Norwich stared at her in horror. "You mean you are not sure? You were pretending?"

"No . . . No, I was not pretending, but I have just not worked out all the details." Allie ignored his answering groan, her mind struggling with those same details.

"Can you at least give me an idea of what you are planning?" he demanded. "After all, you are rather inexperienced. It could be totally impossible!"

Just as Mrs. Montgomery was about to reassure her brother-in-law that she was entirely capable of devising a plan by herself, Jeffers returned and announced that Lord Caston and Mr. Hastings had come to call on her.

Recognizing reinforcements, Allie requested they be shown up.

Reading her mind, Lord Norwich ground out,

"Do you think they will support such a hare-brained idea, Allie. They both know you are not yet up to snuff. You should leave the plotting to us. We will protect you."

"It is my life at stake! I have a right to try to save it! You want me to sit in the parlor doing needlework and pretend that all is well. I cannot do that!"

"Here now," Billy interrupted in alarmed tones, "mustn't fight with a female, old man. Not at all the thing!"

Lord Caston, following in his footsteps, studied the two combatants but said nothing until he had saluted Mrs. Montgomery's hand. "Is everything all right?"

"Yes."

"No!"

The two new arrivals stared first at Mrs. Montgomery and then at the Earl, the unspoken question in their eyes.

Norwich finally capitulated and explained in grim tones, "Lady Jersey was here to invite Allie to her ball tomorrow. Lady Amabel Courtney will also be there."

The listeners looked at each other before Lord Caston ventured, "Surely you refused!"

Allie ignored both her brother-in-law's "Aha!" and the reproof in Caston's eyes. She turned to the only silent member of the trio. "I have a plan."

"Hope you have the right gown to wear. Going to be a mad crush. Everyone wanted to attend. Surprised Sally would invite Lady Amabel, though. Don't like her above half."

"Mr. Hastings . . ." Allie pleaded for his attention.

"Of course she doesn't like her!" Norwich interjected. "She's only invited either of them to provide entertainment for her guests. She's hoping for an historic confrontation!"

"Could be right," Billy agreed meditatively. "Be sure you have the right gown, Mrs. Montgomery. People might talk about this for years. Wouldn't want them to remember you as dowdy."

"Oh, Mr. Hastings!" Allie exclaimed in a cross between a sob and a laugh. Her adviser moved over to sit beside her on the sofa, his pudgy hand gently patting hers.

"That's better. Mustn't look so worried. We'll take care of you."

"That's just the point," Norwich stated triumphantly. "She refuses to allow that. She insists on forming her own plans, and who knows what kind of addlepated scheme she has dreamed up!"

"If you would at least listen instead of raging on, I would tell you!" Allie retorted angrily.

"They're at it again," Billy sighed, looking at a bemused Lord Caston.

"Perhaps we should ring for tea. At least it would give them an opportunity to collect their thoughts," Caston suggested, enjoying the drama being enacted before them in spite of its seriousness. "Or . . . Norwich could sit down and let Mrs. Montgomery explain her plan."

Both men ignored their friend's disgusted look and turned instead to the pleased smile of their hostess.

"Thank you both. You are true gentlemen."

"And I suppose I am not?" Norwich demanded.

"Come, Norwich, sit down and let Mrs. Montgomery tell us her plan."

Disgruntled, the Earl obeyed Caston's command, but his expression told everyone he was doing so under protest.

Mrs. Montgomery, nervous now that she held everyone's attention, began hesitantly, "Well, it is still not quite firm in my mind, but perhaps if I explain it to you, you can help me work it out." She flashed a conciliatory smile at Lord Norwich before continuing. "I thought we would build on the groundwork laid by his lordship. If, in the next two days, he continues his pursuit of Lady Amabel, making her believe he is about to offer for her, and then, when she appears at the ball, he abandons her to come to my side . . ."

Allie peeped at Lord Norwich's face to see his reaction, but he wore a noncommittal mask.

Lord Caston stared into space for a moment. "That would certainly make her angry, but I'm not sure I see how it would expose her role in your husband's murder."

"I haven't thought that far," Allie admitted.

"All it would do is cause her to retreat to Sir Harold and solidify their position," Lord Norwich said grimly.

"Cut off her retreat. That's what Wellington would do."

"What do you mean, Billy?" Lord Caston asked.

Norwich, following his friend's train of thought, said, "That would mean eliminating Sir

Harold. I would certainly not shed a tear at his demise, but I do not wish to go to Newgate to pay for it, my friend."

Allie, listening intently, suddenly beamed. "Of course! That's it! Mr. Hastings, you are brilliant!"

"I am?"

"Yes! If we remove Norwich *and* Sir Harold, she will have no retreat. But the most vulnerable will be Sir Harold. She will be angry and will try to force him back to her side. If left alone, she might even remind him of what she knows. And if we can convince Lady Jersey to leave certain side chambers available and have several influential people in the room next to them to overhear, would it not serve as a confession?"

"That seems most tenuous. How would you know what room they would use and would you be able to get someone in there to listen? It is all too indefinite."

Allie frowned at her brother-in-law. "It may not be perfect, but it has a chance."

"She is right, you know, Norwich," Lord Caston agreed. "But you have not explained how we remove Sir Harold, Mrs. Montgomery."

"Oh, that is the easy part. I shall flirt with him and hint he has a chance to collect both my husband's and my father's fortunes if he plays along. Do you think the bait will be large enough?" she asked anxiously.

"Wouldn't take half that much if you were included," Mr. Hastings assured her gallantly.

"Cut line, Billy! That is impossible, Allie! You are not sophisticated enough for such a ploy!"

"That might be her very attraction, Norwich.

Besides, if the timing is right and Sir Harold thinks Lady Amabel is going to marry you, he will have drunk enough champagne to make the task an easy one."

"It will make the task a disgusting one. I will not have that . . . that rake slobbering all over Allie!"

"Why not? I watched you fawn all over that j-jade!" Allie shouted in return before covering her lips with her hand. Her cheeks inflamed with her embarrassment, she rose swiftly. "I apologize," she whispered before running to the door and out of the room.

"Think it might work," Billy commented calmly, breaking into the stunned silence that followed.

"Don't be so damned ridiculous!"

"Norwich, there's no reason to lose your temper with Billy, here. He's not the one with whom you are angry."

"I shall be angry with him if he continues with such a preposterous plan."

His two friends watched as the Earl paced back and forth across the room, his hands clenched at his side. Only when his pace slowed and one hand was raised, fingers unclenched, to drag through his thick black curls, did they speak again.

"I think Mrs. Montgomery is under a great deal of strain, what with time growing short," Caston began cautiously.

"An understatement," Norwich drawled in disgust.

"Still think it's a good plan," Billy contributed stubbornly.

"You at least owe it to Mrs. Montgomery to sit down and go over her idea logically. After all, men are much better at that than women. Then you can explain clearly to her why it won't work," Caston suggested, giving Billy a wink.

"All right, I will show you that it won't work, but don't blame me when it falls apart before your very eyes."

Both men solemnly agreed to his statement, and all three sat down to discuss the details.

# Chapter Eleven

It galled Lord Norwich that he was unable to find flaws in Mrs. Montgomery's plan. Worse, his friends had left it to him to inform her of their agreement. Of course, they had added some refinements, several of which required the assistance of Lady Jersey, a risky business at best. But he still believed there was great risk for Allie, also. And he did not want her hurt.

In spite of his fears, there was a growing admiration for her courage and determination. She was no ornament, content to observe life from the shelf. She was the kind of woman who would be a companion in life, the kind of woman he had always sought. Visions of her warm brown eyes, her flushed cheeks, her shining smile, only confirmed his thoughts. He would never tire of sharing his life with Allie.

But how did she feel about him? He didn't know and until she was proved innocent, he would be a cad to try to discover her heart. She needed him now, no matter how she felt about him as a man. So he would wait. And after she was free from the shadow hanging over her, he would declare himself.

Now, however, he must inform her of his agreement to her plan. Perhaps, in view of his feelings, it would be better if he kept his distance. Even though it seemed cowardly, he would write her a note. After all, he had quite a lot to do.

His friends were going to consult with Sally Jersey, leaving him free to lay the groundwork with the villainess herself. It would take excellent acting on his part to convince Amabel Courtney of his serious intentions when his mind was filled with thoughts of Allie.

Mrs. Montgomery received his lordship's message from Jeffers himself, an indication of her rising status in the household. With trembling hands, she unfolded the smooth foolscap and studied it. His reluctance was evident in every word, but she believed it was possible to trick Lady Amabel into betraying Sir Harold.

And the thought of being free to live her own life, even if it took her away from Lord Norwich, was a goal for which she could eagerly strive. Another rap on her door interrupted Mrs. Montgomery's thoughts. "Yes?"

A footman informed her that Mr. Browning was awaiting her in the drawing room, and with a quick smoothing down of her hair, she went to meet her unexpected caller.

"Mr. Browning," she greeted him as she swept into the room, "how nice to see you so soon. Do you have additional information?"

"No, madam, I'm sorry to say I do not. I just stopped by to . . . to see if I could be of assistance in any way."

"That is very kind of you. We have just worked out a new plan, and I will tell you about it. Perhaps you will see ways in which to strengthen it." Allie described their scheme, then waited for his response.

"Hmmm, that could work, Mrs. Montgomery, if our suspicions are correct."

"Heavens! I had not thought of that. I have suspected that pair for so long, it never occurred to me we could be wrong."

The stricken look on her face hastened Mr. Browning's reassurance. "Of course we are right, but you must be prepared for every eventuality. I would be glad to assist you if there is anything I can do."

"I can think of nothing, Mr. Browning, other than your prayers."

"Perhaps it would hasten Sir Harold's desertion if word is put about that your father's estate has been settled with more detail than I would normally furnish about its contents."

"But would Sir Harold hear of it in time?"

"I think I could ensure that." Frowning into the distance, Mr. Browning considered his idea from several different directions. "Yes, I think that might help you. Do I have your permission to do so?"

"Yes, of course, Mr. Browning. You have excellent judgment," Allie assured him warmly. "That is all we have left to do, I believe . . . except make sure my wardrobe is adequate to the occasion. Mr. Hastings insisted on that. Oh! Mme Feydeau is making up a silver tissue over gray silk ensemble for me. It would be perfect for the occasion. I wonder if . . . forgive me, Mr. Browning. I did not mean to bore you with ladies' talk."

"No such thing, madam. Shall I stop at Mme Feydeau's and check on the progress of the gown?"

"Perhaps it would be more effective if you took Mavis to check on the gown, Mr. Browning. She is more familiar with female finery," Allie suggested with a smile.

Allie's interest was aroused when she saw Mr. Browning's response. His smile was all out of proportion to her simple suggestion. She rang for a footman and instructed him to send Mavis to the drawing room, prepared for an outing, carefully making no mention of the presence of Mr. Browning.

While waiting for Mavis's appearance, Allie led the conversation into innocuous channels, all the while carefully observing her guest, noting his frequent glances toward the closed door. At the first sign of entrance, he lost all interest in their conversation.

Allie watched as her abigail discovered Mr. Browning's presence in the drawing room.

"Mrs. Montgomery . . . Oh! I did not see you, Mr. Browning. Excuse me, I will—will come back when you are alone, madam."

The flame in her cheeks only intensified as Mr. Browning, already standing, moved toward her, his hand involuntarily extended as if to draw her to him. "Miss Thompson. No, don't leave . . . I mean, Mrs. Montgomery . . ." His words were part explanation and part appeal, and Allie responded.

"Mr. Browning was kind enough to offer to carry out an errand for me, but I believe it calls for your expertise."

"Yes, ma'am."

"I need the silver and gray ball gown Mme Feydeau is making for me for tomorrow evening. Could you go to her shop and plead with her to have it ready by tomorrow afternoon? And could you carry with you my new gray slippers and see if they are the correct shade?"

"Of course," Mavis responded with controlled dignity, purposefully ignoring the still figure who remained standing close to her.

"And Mr. Browning offered to escort you so we would not have to call out Lord Norwich's carriage."

" 'Tisn't necessary. I can manage. I'll just . . ."

"Accompany me. There are several items I need to discuss with you, Miss Thompson. It will save time if we accomplish two errands at the same time."

The beleaguered young woman, after flashing a

panicky look at the gentleman, turned in appeal to Allie but her mistress abandoned Mavis to her fate. "Time is of the essence, Mavis, and you will get there faster with Mr. Browning."

"All right," Mavis agreed in a wooden voice, her face devoid of expression. Turning toward Mr. Browning, she nodded her head and said, "I'll go fetch the slippers." Without further comment, the young woman beat a hasty retreat.

There was silence following her departure, Allie studying her caller and Mr. Browning lost in his own thoughts. Abruptly conscious of Mrs. Montgomery's interest, the gentleman smiled ruefully. "Am I so transparent?"

"A certain interest is noticeable, Mr. Browning."

Her hesitancy registered with the bemused man, and he looked at her sharply. "Do I not have your blessing, madam?"

"That depends on your intent, Mr. Browning. Mavis has not been gently treated by life so far. I would a better future for her."

"Then we are in agreement. I, too, want Miss Thompson to have a happier future. I hope to assist in that future as her husband, if she will have me."

Allie released the breath she had not realized she was holding. "I am pleased, Mr. Browning. I was afraid . . ."

"I know. Lord Norwich suggested—" He halted abruptly.

Allie's chin rose and her lips firmed as she mentally completed his comment. "I have no doubt of that, Mr. Browning, but I am delighted with your solution for Mavis's future. Of course, I have every intention of providing for her and will give her a generous dowry."

Mr. Browning's eyes flashed as he spoke. "That is not necessary, madam. Mavis may come to me as she is. I need no inducement."

"It is because you do not, Mr. Browning, that I am pleased to provide one. I would not have Mavis feel that she comes to you empty-handed. She saved my life in Newgate. You cannot deny me the opportunity to give to her some pride and dignity."

Their eyes met in understanding and the shared love they had for a courageous woman. At that moment that same young woman, dressed in a gray mantle that matched the plainness of her servant's gray gown, returned. Mr. Browning moved to her side, his arm extended, and Mavis gingerly placed her hand on the blue superfine of his coat. With an audacious smile at his hostess, Mr. Browning led the little abigail from the room, commenting over his shoulder, "I will return Miss Thompson to you when we complete our mission."

Allie watched them go with a smile, wondering whether Mavis had any hint of Mr. Browning's intentions. Her mind dwelt on such delicious thoughts until a sense of loneliness stole over her.

In spite of her joy for Mavis, she could not bar the fear of facing life alone should she survive the next three weeks. Underlying her loneliness was her despair at the thought of leaving John . . . Lord Norwich. She could not remain with him once her fate was determined. Nor could she

bear a day to pass without seeing him. Even arguing with him was better than being apart.

Unfortunately, she now knew Lord Norwich's
opinion of Mavis and Mr. Browning's proposed
marriage. Mr. Browning's indiscretion hurt her in
a way he couldn't have known. Should her most
delicious fantasy be fulfilled, and Norwich asked
for her hand in marriage, it, too, would be an
unequal marriage—just like Mavis's and Mr.
Browning's.

Allie's chin unconsciously rose again as she
shook off her slough of despair. Only when her
life was almost taken from her had she learned its
sweetness. She might not have the happiness that
Mavis would enjoy as Mr. Browning's wife, but
she would have her fortune and her freedom. If
that was all the future held for her, she was determined it would be more than sufficient. But
that determination could not stop her from hoping for much more.

Mavis Thompson slid across the seat of the
hackney coach after Mr. Browning had hastily
wiped the dust from it with his handkerchief,
making room for him to follow her inside.

"I'm afraid this is not too elegant . . . Mavis,"
he apologized ruefully.

"No, Mr. Browning, this is just fine. I . . . I
have been in much worse," she added bravely, as
if revealing a terrible secret.

Mr. Browning smiled tenderly down at the
bowed head and tightly clasped hands that were
beginning to show the effects of care. He reached

out a hand to pat Mavis's arm but withdrew it when she flinched. "Those days are past, Mavis."

"Yes . . . for the moment."

"What do you mean, for the moment?"

"We never know where fate will lead us, Mr. Browning. I have no money, no family, no position other than what Mrs. Montgomery has given me out of the kindness of her heart."

"Not out of kindness, Mavis, but out of gratitude and love."

"She doesn't have reason to be grateful to me."

"You helped her in prison."

"Just as she helped me. No, it doesn't bear talking about."

"No, it doesn't. You are alone no longer, Mavis." Mr. Browning frowned as the coach pulled to a halt. It clearly was not the time or place to share his plans with Mavis, but he was becoming impatient with his secret.

"Here ya be, guv'nor," the coachman said as he swung the door open.

Almost half an hour later, the couple reemerged into the crowded streets of London. Mr. Browning led Mavis down the street, intent on his destination. There was an acceptable tearoom in Claridge's where they could share some respectable privacy.

"Mr. Browning, where . . . we need to go in the other direction," Mavis protested in bewilderment.

"First, we must have some refreshment, Mavis. We are going to Claridge's."

"No! I am not dressed for Claridge's, Mr.

Browning. I shall just return to Lord Norwich's, please."

"We cannot do that, Mavis. It is too difficult for us to find a private place to talk. The servants disapprove and it is entirely possible that either Mrs. Montgomery or Lord Norwich will intrude upon us at any moment, sure that I have come to visit with them rather than you."

"But you have . . . haven't you?"

"I need to talk to you, Mavis, and no one else."

"Is it something about Mrs. Montgomery? Has something happened?"

"It concerns her," he assured her with just a twinge of conscience, "and we need to be private."

Mavis acquiesced to his direction, only occasionally studying his intent features as he hurried her along the street. She had been most reluctant to be alone with Mr. Browning again after their last late-night visit. She found herself daydreaming more of late about a liaison with Mr. Browning than traveling to America. It alarmed her that she could be so easily swayed.

Was associating with Society making her soft? She could not deny that Mr. Browning was a fine figure of a man, and forceful too, she thought, as she followed him meekly into Claridge's tearoom.

Once seated at a discreet table, sheltered from the view of others by an intricately carved screen, Mavis sat stiffly upright, her hands folded tightly in her lap, and waited for Mr. Browning's revelations. When he said nothing, however, even after their tea had been served, Mavis's patience evaporated.

"What is it about Mrs. Montgomery? Does she need something? Has something happened to their newest plan? Will it work?"

"Don't worry, Mavis dar— Uh, I'm sure Mrs. Montgomery will be rescued. Norwich is a formidable opponent."

"Then what did you need to tell me?"

Mr. Browning studied Mavis, his gray eyes noting the smooth band of plaited gold hair neatly in place, the slight flush on her creamy cheeks, the brightness of her blue eyes as they puzzled over the problem, and her delightful figure, demurely clad in the gray dress.

He remembered her appearance in Newgate, when he had first seen her, dirty but proud, determined to fight her way. Her outer appearance was more attractive now, but it was the inner core, the strength, loyalty, and courage, that drew Mr. Browning as much as her comeliness.

"Mavis, I want to . . . to discuss your future."

Even as she stared at him in surprise, Mavis's lips firmed. "There is nothing to discuss."

"Yes, there is. You cannot go to America."

"Yes, I can. Haven't you heard of indentured servants? I might even be a cook if they don't want anything fancy. I've been learning from Lord Norwich's cook."

"Your skills are not the problem. It is your appearance." He hesitated as her cheeks flamed and her eyes dropped before continuing. "You have suffered because of men, Mavis; you know what I am talking about. That jailer at Newgate wasn't the only one who wanted you."

Mavis raised her eyes, now a cool blue, and

stared at the man across from her. "There is no place for me here. In England, I will always be a servant. In America, I can become whatever I want."

"How do you know that?"

"Harry's brother wrote him lots about America. It's all the talk belowstairs."

"Who is Harry?" Mr. Browning demanded, afraid he had competition.

"One of Lord Norwich's footmen."

"But you need someone to protect you!"

"I can protect myself!" Mavis responded shakily.

"No, you can't, and I won't let you! I love you!"

The two combatants stared at each other in surprise, their whispered argument forgotten.

Sensing her self-protective withdrawal, Mr. Browning extended his hand across the table. "Mavis, I did not mean to spring it on you like that. But I cannot let you go. I want to protect you, care for you . . ."

Mavis squeezed her eyes shut, frantically fighting the softness that rose within her, the desire for the man sitting opposite her. She had protected her body with every ounce of her being against those who would take what she would not give, but this struggle was the hardest of all because she was fighting herself. "Please, Mr. Browning, you mustn't."

"Yes, I must, Mavis. I admire you so much. We can have such happiness. I have been lonely most of my life, sweetheart. I cannot bear the thought of going on without you."

A single tear slipped past her tightly shut lids and slid down her cheek before it was lifted from her face by Mr. Browning's finger. Resting there, the glistening bubble of moisture held his eyes as he said softly, "I did not mean to make you cry, sweetheart. Can you not feel anything for me?"

When there was no response, Mr. Browning withdrew his hand, his heart heavy. "It is all right, Mavis. I will not importune you again. I am rather old, I know, and probably staid compared to others you have known. It . . . it was just a dream. I realize . . ."

"No! No! I am honored, Mr. Browning. But I can't!"

"You can't, Mavis?" the man questioned.

"Don't you see? If I let you care for me now, then when you are tired of me, I will be too soft and afraid. I cannot."

"Tired of you?" Mr. Browning demanded, a mixture of horror and anger dominating his tones as he realized what Mavis believed.

"Mr. Browning, I am just a poor girl, uneducated and untrained. You are a man of the world and you will soon tire of me. There are others younger and prettier than me. I've seen too many streetwalkers dying in poverty. I—I vowed I'd not live my life like that." Tears were now coursing freely down her face as Mavis raised tragic blue eyes to face him.

Mr. Browning ignored her appeal, his anger overriding his tender heart. Throwing a handful of pound notes on the table, he rose from his chair and grasped Mavis by the arm, lifting her from her chair and drawing her after him in one smooth motion. Mavis, too surprised by his action to protest, scrambled to get her feet under her before he dragged her across the floor.

Outside, his abrupt motion for a hackney coach was instantly obeyed, and as he bundled her inside willy-nilly, the coachman leaned down to ask, "Where to, guv?"

"Anywhere! Just keep driving until I tell you to stop!"

The coachman grinned and set his cob horse off at a leisurely pace to traverse the crowded London streets, heading for a park where he could enjoy his work and hopefully receive a fat fee.

Inside, Mavis huddled into a corner waiting for her companion's anger to recede. She was not sure why he was angry. He had not seemed angry when she had turned him down, only hurt. That had wrung her heart. It was only afterward, when she was trying to explain her reasons that he had lost his temper.

After several deep breaths, the normally calm Mr. Browning regained control of his senses, and he turned to Mavis. "Forgive me for treating you so roughly, but it never occurred to me you thought I was asking you to become my mistress. I . . . I had thought of you as my wife for several days now, and it just never occurred to me that you were not in tune with my thoughts."

"No, no, no! I could not do that to . . . No!"

"But, Mavis . . ." he began when he saw that tears were again falling from her eyes. "Sweetheart, don't cry, please!"

"I cannot. I love you, Mr. Browning, but I cannot . . ."

Timothy, always a man of thought rather than action, spared no time for such an occupation once his love had confessed her feelings. Grasping her shoulders, he pulled her to him, his lips seeking the full lips, his body the soft warmth of hers. Mavis, long resistant to such persuasion, melted at his touch, her body aching for him as she moved even closer.

Several minutes passed in such delightful occupation before the staid Mr. Browning took control over the masterful Timothy and removed his love from his lap back to the decorous hackney seat, though he did keep her pressed to his side with an arm around her shoulders. "Ah, sweet Mavis, I have longed to hold you so. We must be married very soon."

"No!" she repeated, as if the past five minutes had never taken place.

"What? Why did you say no?" Mr. Browning questioned impatiently, wanting to continue with his plans now that he knew Mavis loved him.

"I cannot marry you," she said quietly.

Silence followed her announcement while Mr. Browning sought for a controlled response. "Why not?" he finally asked.

"Because I understand enough about Society to know it would hurt you. And I love you. Enough to not want to do that."

"Why would it hurt me?" he questioned in almost unemotional tones, the staid Mr. Browning back in control of the impulsive Timothy.

"I am not the proper wife for a man of business. People like Lord Norwich would take away their business. They don't like people to overstep their places."

Mr. Browning thought long and hard about what Mavis had said. There was an element of truth in it, but he had considered it worth the risk to have Mavis by his side. But he realized such acceptance would not reassure the young woman beside him. It was those qualities he most admired in her that would prevent her from accepting his proposal if she thought it would hurt him in any way. So he did not attempt to persuade her she was wrong. Instead, he looked for alternatives.

"I cannot disagree with you, sweetheart," he began, causing Mavis's heart to sink, "but neither can I give up the idea of making you my wife. While there might be some who would refuse to employ me, I feel it would be worth the risk."

"No," she said with a sob.

Smiling warmly, he drew her head against his shoulder. "Somehow I felt that would be your response. Now, we must put our minds to this and between the two of us, I am sure we will find an answer, because I refuse to give you up. You are mine, now, bound to me by your kisses, your vow of love, and mine you will stay."

"But, Mr. Browning—"

"Timothy, love, Timothy."

"Timothy," she began shyly, "I do not see how. If this were America, no one would think badly of me or you, but it is England."

"That is it!"

Mavis's head came up as her love exclaimed and hugged her to him. "What?"

"We will go to America together!"

In spite of the bound her beleaguered heart took, Mavis protested, "No, Timothy, you cannot do that. What would happen to your work?"

"It is all so simple. Why did I not think of it earlier?" he wondered. "Don't you see, Mavis? Like many gentlemen, Lord Norwich has holdings in America, and all of them must deal with men they have never met, entrust them with great wealth. Why not go to America as an agent for the ton? I have a good reputation, and I'm sure Lord Norwich would far rather deal with me than with an unknown, and he can recommend me to others."

"Do you think he would?" Mavis asked, hope rising in her voice.

"I'm sure of it, love! We'll make our own fortune in America. Oh, Mavis! It is wonderful! I had not realized how confined I felt here until now!"

"You're not doing this just for me?"

Mr. Browning looked down into her anxious face and tenderly stroked her cheek before lifting her chin so that his lips could meet hers in a gentle salute. "Mavis, love, you would be worth much more, but I sincerely want to go to America, with you at my side, and conquer the New World. We will find a large house and have lots of children, with shining gold hair, all born of our love, and they will have the opportunity to be whatever they want, because you are their mother."

Mavis subsided against Timothy, content for the moment to savor the future as pictured by her companion. It was almost too much for her to comprehend. Her life had changed so dramatically in the past several months. To have happiness rise from such despair was incomprehensible.

"We will tell Mrs. Montgomery as soon as we return," Mr. Browning continued, his gray eyes bright as his planning gained speed.

"Yes, we . . . Oh, no! Timothy, we mustn't!"

"Why not, love?"

"I cannot abandon her before she is freed. If she should not . . . if something goes wrong, I must stay by her side."

Timothy hugged her to him once more. "Of course, you are right, love. I had forgotten Mrs. Montgomery's problem. We will say nothing until her fate has been determined. But I hope and pray it is settled at that ball tomorrow night! I do not feel I can wait much longer!"

Mavis did not use words to confirm her agreement. She simply moved back into his arms, bringing his lips to hers, prepared to pour out all the love she had hoarded for so many years.

Meanwhile, the driver of their hackney was spending a delightful afternoon touring the park, smacking his lips at the prospect of the large fee he was surely earning.

# Chapter Twelve

Lord Norwich ascended the steps to Lady Jersey's town house in the wake of Lady Amabel Courtney, his head bowed as he carefully reviewed their plan. It had been a difficult two days since they had determined their path. The only good news was that his stepmother had suffered a nervous collapse and withdrawn to recuperate at Brighton. While he pitied her, it removed one threat to Mrs. Montgomery. But he feared it would be the only danger removed this night.

In spite of his valiant efforts to play his role, and he thought he had been moderately successful, he had no confidence in solving their problem this evening. Certainly, Lady Amabel had given every indication she would accept his declaration if he were so foolish as to offer for her, and Sir Harold had been alienated by her devotion to him. Nevertheless, she was as shrewd as they came, and he had no faith in her losing her temper and giving away the game. And he himself was concerned with freeing Allie from the threat of the gallows to begin making plans for her . . . their future.

Lady Amabel threw an inviting smile over her shoulder to him and Lord Norwich responded automatically. She was the proverbial cat licking the cream this evening, reveling in her invitation to one of *the* social events of the season. For the past several years, the haughty matrons of Almack's had excluded her.

She believed her renewed acceptance came as a

direct result of Lord Norwich's patronage, and this had given her an even greater incentive to attain marriage with him. However, she had not quite been able to bring herself to abandon her mourning, or at least the trappings of mourning. Though black in color, the cut of her dress was immodest, not the garb of a grieving widow.

When they reached the top of the stairs, Lady Amabel received her first surprise of the evening. Lady Jersey greeted her coldly, almost to the point of rudeness. She barely faltered at the offense, but she drew closer to Lord Norwich as her protector, and also her entrée to such select society. Lord Norwich hardened his heart against her distress and greeted Lady Jersey with his customary friendliness.

Norwich waited for Lady Amabel to comment on Lady Jersey's behavior after they moved into the main ballroom, but she chose to ignore it, much to his relief. Following in their footsteps was Sir Harold, a determined third in their party. He, too, had been greeted frostily by his hostess, and his glowering visage did not invite greetings from casual acquaintances.

Already the large room was growing crowded, a sure sign of success. Lady Amabel preened under the attention she was drawing, but her delighted smile froze as she was snubbed by the dowagers and young matrons in her path. Only the men in attendance seemed to welcome her.

As planned, Lord Norwich gave no notice of such behavior, continuing to stroll about the room and greet acquaintances. As they drew up beside a column gaily decorated with garlands of flowers, a murmur rose from the growing crowd and the trio turned back toward the entrance to see what new arrival had drawn such interest.

Lord Norwich grimaced. This had not been planned, but Society's response to Mrs. Montgomery's arrival promised success for the evening. Her silver skirts swayed softly as she leaned on the arm of her escort, Lord Caston, with Mr. Hastings in close attendance. She reminded Lord Norwich of a shining star, twinkling in the distance, its fragile light drawing all eyes. He only wished he were beside her.

Lady Amabel, eclipsed by her enemy, gritted her teeth in frustration. She was determined to give her rival a comeuppance in Society as well as in the courts. As her mind sought a way, she was handed the answer by Mrs. Montgomery herself. While she watched the young woman surrounded by many of the social lights eager to meet her, she saw the little widow survey the room until her gaze fell on Norwich. Instinctively, Lady Amabel drew closer to the Earl and the fire in her rival's eyes confirmed the chit's weakness. The girl was in love with Norwich! Already encouraged to believe the Earl was there for the taking, Lady Amabel determined she'd get him to declare for her before the evening ended.

Lord Norwich had seen Mrs. Montgomery's response to his companion. Her reaction filled him with pleasure until he reminded himself it was merely playacting for their plan. After all, it gave Lady Amabel the incentive to encourage him rather than the glowering Sir Harold. But if Allie's jealousy was real, it gave an added boost to his hopes. He reluctantly dampened his eagerness. There was no time for introspection now.

Sir Harold watched the notorious widow's entrance. Mr. Browning had done his work well, and it had come to Sir Harold's ear that Mrs. Montgomery, besides inheriting her husband's estate, consisting mainly of her dowry and some encumbered pieces of real estate, had inherited her merchant father's vast fortune.

He watched the young bucks surround the widow, knowing many of them had heard the same information and were interested in feathering their nests. He should have pursued her rather than Lady Amabel, he told himself bitterly. He would have received ten times the fortune and have to split it with no one.

Once the music began, the crowds formed and re-formed after each dance, and Allie met more people than she could possibly remember. The whirl of beautiful gowns, the glitter of jewels, the laughter and whispering, the champagne and the feast prepared in the dining room, all became a beautiful blur. Only Lady Amabel and Lord Norwich, always together, stood out. Allie's eyes followed them as they moved around the ballroom.

Once, strolling with a young man, a polite but hopeless coxcomb, Allie actually bumped into Lord Norwich and his companion. The glare she gave her brother-in-law while ignoring Lady Amabel only added fuel to the fire. In spite of the snubs she received, Lady Amabel was enjoying herself immensely. More and more she ignored Sir Harold and clung to Lord Norwich.

Sir Harold, angered by his co-conspirator's be-havior, drank champagne recklessly. When Lord Norwich and Lady Amabel, late in the evening, sat down on a settee that left no room for him, he wandered off into a small salon set aside for the guests who grew tired of the dance floor. Finding himself alone, he slumped into a chair, his hand holding his aching head.

Lord Caston, keeping an eye on their target while Allie danced with Mr. Hastings, greeted them as they stepped from the floor with the knowledge that the time had come for action.

With a wide-eyed acknowledgment and a de-termined nod, Allie moved toward the salon.

"We'll be close by, Mrs. Montgomery. Just scream if you need us."

Allie acknowledged their whispered reassur-ance with a nod but continued on her way. Just before entering, she withdrew a lacy handker-chief from her reticule and held it to her eyes. Moving into the dim light, she pulled the door behind her and turned around sniffling into her handkerchief. Ignoring her quarry slumped over in one of the wing-back chairs, she moaned loudly.

Sir Harold, roused from his drunken depression by the sound, turned his head to discover Mrs. Montgomery standing several yards from him, crying softly. Struggling to his feet, he moved away from the woman rather than to her.

Allie gasped and whirled around to face him. "Oh! I . . . I thought I was alone." She moved several steps closer, raising her brown eyes ap-pealingly. "I didn't mean to disturb you."

"No—no, of course not. Didn't disturb me," he assured her.

"It is just that I cannot stay there and watch him submit to that—woman's . . . Oh! I should not be saying that to you. You are her friend, are you not?" Again she moved several steps closer, her silver dress gleaming in the firelight.

"I know her," Sir Harold admitted gruffly.

"I thought he liked me a little, but now I know he was only playing me along. It is Lady Amabel he really loves. I think he is going to marry her!" Allie traversed the remaining distance between them.

Sir Harold stared at the vision before him, finding her an attractive woman, the modest cut of her gown more stirring than the flamboyance of Lady Amabel's attire. In addition, his befuddled mind laboriously recalled her wealth. He struggled for the words that would draw her to him.

"He would be a fool to choose her over you."

"But she's so beautiful!"

"She's rotten inside."

"But it is rumored you and she—"

"I was Montgomery's friend, that's all! I could be your friend, too. He would want that," he assured her with labored breathing. What sweet revenge on Edward! He'd always envied him for his family connections. And revenge on Belle too, she who had scorned his advances until she needed him.

But now she had abandoned him for a richer prize: Montgomery's brother. How appropriate if he married the despised little widow and snatched her fortune.

Allie's lashes fluttered demurely before she looked back up at him, her brown eyes soft in the firelight. "Sir Harold," she said breathlessly, "I would be honored if you would be my friend."

Sir Harold reached out to take her hand and draw it to his thick lips as she innocently pressed toward him like a small puppy seeking warmth.

Lord Norwich, sitting out a country dance with Lady Amabel, sighed, wondering how much longer he would have to endure the woman, when he saw Lord Caston give the signal. Anxiously, he glanced about the room. This was the critical moment and he was filled with foreboding at the idea of Mrs. Montgomery's being alone with Sir Harold.

He saw Lady Jersey respond to Mr. Hastings's whispered alert and approach the couple. When the music ended, Lady Jersey drew Lord Norwich away. To Lady Amabel it looked as if the two of them were arguing. The next thing she knew, an angry Lord Norwich was gripping her arm and forcing her toward the door. "We must depart now, Belle."

"Depart? Are you foxed? It is still early!"

"Nevertheless, it seems you . . . we have worn out our welcome."

"What are you saying?"

"Some of the guests object to your presence."

"Did Lady Jersey ask you to take me away?" she demanded in fierce anger.

"Yes."

"Well, we will show her how much her wishes

mean! I think I *will* dance, after all, Lord Norwich!"

"No, I think not."

Amabel stared at the Earl for several minutes
before she demanded, "Do you care what she
says?"

"Yes, I do, Belle. I'm sorry. It has been fun, the
past week, but I have no intention of risking my
reputation for you."

"But you want me! I know you do! You cannot . . ." she sputtered, but she ran out of words
as she saw cold disinterest wash over his face.

An all-consuming anger rose up within her as
she realized she had been dropped. Without another word, she turned and rushed away, her furious blue eyes seeking Sir Harold among the
crush of guests.

Several people, standing nearby, had been
coached by Lord Caston and Mr. Hastings as to
the location of Sir Harold, so Lady Amabel experienced no difficulty at all in discovering which
room held her partner in crime.

The moment Lady Amabel had moved to the
next point in their campaign, Lord Norwich was
joined by Lord Caston. "Good news," his friend
whispered. "Mr. Browning came to the house just
before we departed. Your man identified Sir Harold's valet as the servant at your brother's house
and the Bow Street Runners have taken him into
custody."

"Excellent! The sooner this is over, the happier
I will be. Where is Billy?"

"He is organizing several respected members of

the government in the next room to witness. For whatever reason, the room has three peepholes that give the gentlemen an excellent observation post for whatever happens next."

"Let's join them. I fear for Mrs. Montgomery. She is unaware of how beastly the man can be."

"Not to mention Lady Amabel. She didn't look pleased when she left you."

With a motion for silence, Caston led the way into the little salon.

Just as Allie steeled herself to accept Sir Harold's repulsive kiss, Lady Amabel Courtney burst into the room, and discovered the pair silhouetted before the fireplace.

"Harry! Who . . . It's you!" Her shriek of rage shook Allie's confidence in her ability to carry out her part, but she drew a deep breath and stayed where she was.

"What do you want, Belle? You're not needed here. Go back and play with your Earl."

"What are you talking about, Harry?" Lady Amabel demanded in a hard voice. "We're . . . partners, remember?" Her meaning was not lost on him.

"Not anymore. I don't think I want to be partners with a double-crosser like you."

"I haven't double-crossed you! Nothing's changed. We're going to bring it off."

"No! I don't think so. I've got other plans, now."

"Is that why you're cozying up to that . . . that baggage? You lily-livered coward! She'll never marry you!"

"Perhaps I had better wait in the ballroom, Sir Harold," Allie offered tentatively. "When you have finished your discussion, will you join me?" The fluttering of her lashes and the shy smile were a clear invitation and he eagerly agreed. It was best she leave and not hear the incriminating things Lady Amabel was sure to say in her present state.

As Allie attempted to slip from the room, Lady Amabel grabbed her arm and spun her around. "Oh, no, you don't. You'll stay right here and listen to me."

"Belle, keep your mouth shut!"

"No! I will not be beaten by a merchant's daughter! She will listen to me!" Turning to a pale Allie, she added viciously, "The man you just so sweetly invited to dance killed your husband!"

"Belle!" Sir Harold roared as he moved toward the two women. "You'll not tell tales on me and stay lily-pure yourself. You planned it when you discovered Montgomery would not bend to your will. You're not going to shift the blame on me!"

"Be quiet, you fool! I suffered Edward's cruel treatment too long to give up now," the blond woman cried, real pain in her voice.

Allie, hoping to escape during their argument, shifted silently toward the door. "No you don't!" Sir Harold warned, reaching for her. Allie shrank from his touch, no longer willing to pretend.

"Please, leave me alone!"

"Don't listen to her, Mrs. Montgomery. I didn't kill your husband. He was my friend."

"You're not going to turn her up sweet now,

Harry. She won't believe you, no matter how much you protest."

"But I didn't kill him, and you know it."

"Of course you didn't. You had your man do it, and a pretty penny it cost us, too. If you'd had any gumption at all, we wouldn't be paying blackmail money right now."

Allie strained against the tight hold Sir Harold had on her arm, but she could not break free. "She might have believed me if you hadn't insisted on telling her everything. Now what are we going to do with her?"

Lady Amabel stared scornfully at Allie's whitened features. "Perhaps she has become so depressed she commits suicide?" she suggested, an evil smile forming on her face. "Yes, I think that would be appropriate, with a letter confessing to her crime. That would let us off the hook."

"I'm not going to kill her, Belle. I can't do it."

"A coward as usual, Harry?"

Sir Harold ignored her sarcastic tones. "Words can't hurt me, Belle. I don't see you doing any of the dirty work."

"Never mind!" she said impatiently. "I'll take care of your little friend. I'll take great pleasure in it. Let's take her to my house. We'll force her to write the note and then we'll see."

Allie's heart pounded wildly. She sent up a silent prayer that nothing had gone wrong and her friends were listening in the next room. She was ready to be rescued.

As if on cue, the door swung open and Lord Norwich and Lord Caston entered. There was a stricken silence as the culprits tried to assess their chances.

"Why, John, I thought you wanted nothing more to do with me," Lady Amabel purred, moving between Allie and Sir Harold and the newcomers. "Have you changed your mind?"

"No, madam, I have not, particularly not after hearing your confession."

"Confession? What confession?" Lady Amabel's voice lost its soft tones and took on a hardness laced with fear.

"We have just overheard you and your partner admit everything. You and Sir Harold will hang for killing my brother."

Allie, her arm still in Sir Harold's grip, realized it would not be as simple as planned. Sir Harold pulled her over in front of him and grasped her around the waist with his left hand while his right pulled a pistol from his coat.

"You'll not hang me before you bury your pretty little widow here," he growled, the gun pointed at Allie's head. Lady Amabel, never slow to press an advantage, moved behind her partner, using him as a barrier between her and the two men.

Lord Norwich froze as he realized Allie's peril. "Will you hide behind a petticoat, Sir Harold?" he scorned, not moving.

"That's right, my lord. Much better a petticoat than a noose. Now, move away from that door."

Lord Norwich and Lord Caston exchanged glances and reluctantly complied. They watched in frustration as Allie was dragged to the door, her face white, her eyes large with fear.

"Harry! We can't drag her through the middle of the ballroom! We'll never make it!"

"Do you have any better ideas? I don't plan to surrender and be hanged!"

"Wait a minute. Let me think." Lady Amabel stood in silence for a moment while Sir Harold held Allie clutched against him, his hand biting into her waist, the cold steel of the pistol pressed against her temple.

"We'll have to leave England. We can try the Continent. We'll need funds," Lady Amabel planned, her mind reviewing the obstacles. "Gentlemen," she addressed the two standing across from them, "empty your pockets, and Lord Norwich, I'll take that sapphire stickpin. Lord Caston, your ring will have to suffice. Now!" she screamed when they made no move to obey. "Or we'll finish this little charade right here with an end to your precious little sister-in-law!"

The two men reluctantly drew forth what funds and jewelry they had and held it out to the woman.

"No. Toss it over here."

They complied and watched as she counted the notes. "Well, you two are certainly prepared for whatever might take your fancy. We have enough here to live for quite a while, Harry. And . . ." Reaching over to Mrs. Montgomery, she yanked the diamond necklace and earrings off her with no regard to the pain it caused. "This should make us very comfortable."

"Hurry, Belle! I want to get out of here!"

"All right, Harry. You go first with her. Tell

everyone to get back. We'll leave by the front entrance, just the way we came in."

"Right." With a yank to Allie, the trio moved to the door, Lady Amabel opening it before stepping back quickly. Billy and several other men were waiting outside, but once they saw the danger to Mrs. Montgomery, they fell back to allow free passage. Lord Norwich and Lord Caston followed swiftly as the threesome moved into the ballroom, but there was nothing they could do.

Allie, watching her hope of rescue evaporate, struggled against Sir Harold's hold, but it was too tight for her to escape. As the ballroom crowd parted, several women screamed and one lady fainted at the feet of her partner, unnoticed, as he stared at the bizarre parade. Sir Harold motioned to Mr. Hastings. "Go out there and tell them to let us through or I'll put a hole in her head."

Allie moaned and shut her eyes tightly. Then she resumed the struggle against her captor. "Be still, woman, or I'll knock you senseless." She subsided against him. At least, if she were conscious, she might be able to help herself.

"Belle, get a hackney," Sir Harold whispered, as they neared the front door, and the woman hurried down the steps, where a crowd was beginning to gather. Once the hackney was secured, she called to her partner and he shoved Allie inside, crawling after her as he ordered the driver to spring them.

The hackney driver, frightened by the sight of Harold's pistol, did not hesitate, though he had no idea where his passengers wanted to go in such a hurry. Allie, thrown to one side by the rough ride, tried to open the door, but she was thwarted by Amabel.

"Oh, no, you don't, my dear! We still have some use for you!"

"Where shall we go, Belle? They'll head for all the ports."

"What about that connection you have with the freetraders? They could get us across."

"Of course, why didn't I think of that!" He rapped on the rocking carriage's trap door. "North, man, head north!" He settled back in his seat. "When we get to the edge of town, I'll make him get down and I'll drive. If we hire a coach, they'll discover us." He paused before adding, "What about her? We don't need her anymore. Why don't we just put her out? Once she is found, Norwich won't be that determined to catch us."

"No! I'm going to pay back a few debts I owe her!"

"Belle! You can't mean to . . ."

"Oh yes, I can. And you'd better do as I tell you, or I'll find a way to get rid of you, too."

The large man settled back in his seat, his fear of this madwoman evident, and Allie could not blame him. She, too, was terrified.

# Chapter Thirteen

Sir Harold's hopes of passing unnoticed through the London streets soon faded. The sight of a hackney coach that had seen better days pulled by a cob ready for retirement racing as if chased by the hounds of hell was not easily ignored.

When Lord Norwich and Lord Caston called up the Earl's carriage and followed the hackney, they had no difficulty discovering their direction. Pulled by four well-bred 'uns, it did not take long before their quarry was in sight. Each took one of the pair of pistols kept in the carriage, and Mr. Hastings, jumping into the carriage at the last minute, borrowed a blunderbuss from one of the coachmen.

"How shall we overcome them?" Lord Caston asked, as he swayed with the lurching carriage. "I'm afraid we might injure Mrs. Montgomery."

Before Lord Norwich could answer, they drew closer to the hackney as it approached the outer edges of the city. "I believe it is stopping!" he exclaimed. Leaning out of the window, he called to his coachman, "Slow down, Robinson. Make as little noise as possible." He cautioned the others to silence and waited anxiously for them to draw nearer the other coach.

They were aided by the fact that Sir Harold and his hackney driver were by now involved in a heated argument over possession of the vehicle.

Allie, silent in her corner during the wild ride, realized it was up to her to escape. There would be no Mr. Browning coming to bring news and cheer her up, no Lord Norwich to effect a dramatic rescue. Since she was not creating a disturbance, neither of her captors had thought it necessary to tie her, so she remained free. Once the carriage stopped and Sir Harold descended to inform the driver he had reached the end of his ride, Allie watched Lady Amabel without moving.

After a casual glance in her direction, Lady Amabel became engrossed in the fight going on outside. Allie seized her chance and with a swift downward movement, she released the catch on the door and gave Lady Amabel a healthy shove. The woman, caught by surprise, tumbled down onto the roadway, struck her head on a stone, and lay silent.

Allie wasted no time. Before slipping out the other door, she scooped up Lady Amabel's reticule. Not only would it stop the two of them from living off Lord Caston and Lord Norwich and prevent them from selling the jewels, but it would also provide funds for Allie to return to Lord Norwich's town house.

When the pursuers were close enough to see Lady Amabel tumble into the road, they jumped from their carriage and hurried to the hackney coach. Sir Harold, still fighting with the burly coachman, was surprised to find himself pulled around and with a solid right delivered to his jaw.

Lord Norwich ignored the coachman's thanks as he spun around to the carriage door, searching inside for Allie. When he saw the other door open, he shouted "She's gone!" before racing

around to the other side of the carriage. "Allie?
Allie!" he roared as he ran toward the trees that
lined the road.

Allie, trying to untangle her skirts from a
bramble bush, heard that familiar voice and almost fainted with relief. "Here! John? I'm here!"
With a frantic tug, she ripped her skirt free and
turned back to the path she had taken into the
forest. "John? Please . . . please come! I'm
here!"

Each followed the sound of the other's voice.
Allie came out of the forest just as John reached
its edge. There was no hesitation on Allie's part
when he rescued her this time. She flew into his
arms, sobbing ecstatically, and Lord Norwich
hugged her tightly to him. "Are you all right, Allie?" he whispered, never loosening his hold.

"Yes! Yes, but . . . she was going to kill me. I
was so frightened, John!"

He pulled her even closer if possible. "You are
safe now, sweet Allie. They cannot hurt you anymore."

"John? Where are you? Is Mrs. Montgomery all
right?" Mr. Hastings's voice called through the
darkness.

"Yes, Billy, we're coming. And Mrs. Montgomery is just fine."

Allie slept late the next morning. It had been
almost dawn by the time they returned to Lord
Norwich's home after turning the villains over to
the magistrate. Allie had crawled into bed after
receiving a congratulatory hug from a drowsy
Mavis and had not stirred since.

Lord Norwich, on the other hand, had an early morning meeting with Mr. Browning in the library. The first order of events was to review the previous evening's adventure and assure Mr. Browning that his unfailing faith in Mrs. Montgomery had been vindicated.

"A certain personage assures me that no charges will be brought against her. She is now a free woman."

"And a wealthy one, my lord," Browning added.

"Yes," Lord Norwich mused. "I'm sure she'll find herself the desire of many gallants looking for a rich young widow."

"Sir, I'm quite sure Mrs. Montgomery will be equally prized for her beauty and good nature!" Browning added.

"Ah yes. You're right once again," Lord Norwich agreed, and quickly changed the subject to Browning's planned marriage. "You will continue to act as my man of business, will you not?"

"I was not sure you would want me to when I take Miss Thompson as my wife," Mr. Browning said stiffly.

"Don't be foolish, man. I wasn't talking about myself when I suggested you not marry the woman. I was referring to the ton."

"I am pleased to hear that, my lord. I thought . . ."

"No. I am not so narrow-minded as that. But . . . not everyone sees it that way."

"No. But I have heard that in America a man is judged by his abilities, not by his bloodline."

"To some extent that is true. Though they are

not above appreciating civilized behavior and the social graces of the ton." Something in Mr. Browning's expression brought Lord Norwich up short. "You are not thinking of emigrating, are you?"

"Yes, we are. Miss Thompson had intended to go to America alone, but I cannot allow that. She does not feel she can remain here as my wife. So the obvious solution is to go to America together."

"But your business! How will you survive?"

"That is what I intended to discuss with you. After all, you have extensive holdings in America. Would you not prefer to have a man you know handle your investments, rather than someone you have never met?"

"You? Yes, of course I would. But I need you here."

"Nonsense. There are many efficient men of business in the City. I will give you the names of several for you to consider before I leave. And if you recommend me to your friends who have investments in America, I believe I can provide for myself and my wife."

"Without doubt, man, but are you sure you want to abandon all you have built for yourself here for the sake of a woman?"

"Not just any woman, my lord, but for Miss Thompson I would readily give up everything. She is brave, loyal, and sweet. Together we can face anything, and enjoy life the better because it is shared."

Lord Norwich studied the happiness written across Browning's face and wondered how he could have thought the man would be sacrificing anything. He had clearly found more than he would ever give up.

Calling for Jeffers, he instructed him to deliver Mr. Browning to the drawing room where he would await Miss Thompson. If Jeffers was surprised at the prospect of Mrs. Montgomery's abigail entertaining a caller there, he did not show it.

Left alone in the library for a few minutes, Lord Norwich had the opportunity to reconsider his decision. The happiness he had just seen shared by Browning and Mavis had convinced him. Surely if Browning had the fortitude to defy convention for the woman he loved, he—an Earl, a nobleman who could trace his lineage to the Norman conquerors—must do as much. He had held his feelings on a tight rein as long as there had been the slightest hint that the little chit could be a murderer—as if the world weren't well rid of his brother in any case. Imagine! Edward had looked into those brown eyes and innocent face and considered only how to exploit her fortune! But then, he reminded himself, Edward had always been a fool.

Lord Norwich was roused from his thoughts when Jeffers returned with Mrs. Montgomery. Allie had dressed for the interview in her new lilac gown with the violet braid trim and Mavis had arranged her chestnut hair in a braided coronet.

"You wished to see me, my lord?" she said politely, as if last night's embrace had never happened. He was suddenly seized by the fear that it had been only a natural reaction to one who had saved her life, nothing more. He returned to his usual formal manner, although he ached to hold her as she seated herself on the sofa.

"Yes, madam, there are several matters we need to discuss. First, I believe there will be some changes necessary in the way we have conducted matters here."

Allie looked up at him. She, too, was having second thoughts. Was this new stiffness a sign that the Earl wanted to forget about last night? Had he merely been doing his duty and now was anxious to get her out of his house? Very well, she was prepared to give as good as she got.

"Yes, my lord. I will begin looking into a new residence today. Perhaps you have some suggestions about an appropriate address?"

"What are you talking about, Allie?" he said. "There's no need for you to leave here."

"But you said changes. Naturally, since I'm no longer in your custody, I can understand why you would not want to have me here."

"That's not the changes I meant. It's Mavis. Surely you know about her and Browning?"

"Of course, I know of Mr. Browning's intentions. And you made it clear how you felt about them."

Allie's bitter words took Lord Norwich by surprise. "What do you mean?" he asked in confusion.

Allie, embarrassed at her slip, blushed and fumbled for words. "I . . . I don't know what I meant. Excuse me. I must begin packing."

"Packing? Where are you going?" he demanded.

"I cannot stay here now that my future is settled. I will find somewhere to live. Mr. Browning can . . . oh, no, I will find somewhere else on my own."

"You cannot set up house by yourself! Consider your reputation, a young woman alone!"

"I am a widow, my lord, as you well know. And I will find someone to live with me."

"Who?" he demanded jealously.

"It doesn't matter. I'm sure I can find someone decent to give me company."

"This is madness, woman! What is the rush? We cleared your name this morning, and already you are packing your bags? Have you been so unhappy here?"

Allie turned her back on Lord Norwich to hide the tears filling her brown eyes. "No! No, I have not, but I cannot continue to live here."

Norwich pulled her back to face him. "Why are you crying? What have I done to make you cry?"

Allie shook her head in despair. "It is not your fault, my lord. It is just that I must go."

"My lord? Last night you called me John. Why so formal now?" His blue eyes caressed her features.

"Because I am not your equal! That is why you disapproved of Mr. Browning marrying poor Mavis! And that is why I must go."

"I did not think it would be the wisest move for Browning's career."

"So you thought he should take her as his mistress! Is that what you will recommend for me too? That I be some lord's mistress? Because we both know I'm not good enough to marry an aristocrat. Unless, of course, his pockets are to let, and he would suffer marriage to a merchant's daughter in order to fill them!" she said bitterly.

Her anger surprised Lord Norwich. His brother had injured her more deeply than he had thought. "Allie," he said tenderly, "you are worthy of any aristocrat. And I would *never* countenance your being some man's mistress. I have nothing against Mavis or her marriage to Mr. Browning. I only thought to warn him because Polite Society can be very intolerant."

"Mavis is worth ten Amabel Courtneys, and yet she would be snubbed by one and all, while Lady Amabel was welcomed everywhere!"

"Well, not everywhere, Allie, but . . ."

"Oh! You know what I mean!"

"Yes, love, I do, but don't get so upset. It is just the rules of society. We cannot change them for Mavis's sake. I admit I was wrong about their marriage. Their solution is much better."

"Yes, it is. Perhaps I will travel to America also. If Mavis and Mr. Browning can start a new life there, perhaps I can too."

"You have already been accepted here, Allie. There is no need for you to go to America. Any man would be lucky to have you as his wife."

Allie stared up at him with large brown eyes swimming in tears. She did not care about any man. She cared only about this one. Bowing her head, she said in a resigned voice, "Nevertheless, I believe I shall go to America."

"No!" Lord Norwich protested, grasping Allie by the shoulders and shaking her. "I will not let you go without me!" He halted his oration to try a more persuasive technique. His lips covered hers and his arms wrapped themselves around her slender figure, molding her body to his. The sweet caress of his lips was all Allie had imagined it would be, and she yielded to the temptations he offered.

When Lord Norwich, breathing heavily, released her, Allie, though dazed, was not yet prepared to surrender.

"Allie . . . Allie . . ." Lord Norwich whispered hoarsely, his mouth descending again to its newfound partner.

"No! No, John, we mustn't . . ."

"Why mustn't we? Do you not like me to kiss you?"

"Yes . . . yes, I like it very much, but . . . but there is no future in it. I will not become your mistress."

Lord Norwich, after an initial start, pressed Allie's body closer to his, a warm smile on his face. "Yes, you will, my love," he assured her as her heart sank, "you will become my mistress, my love, and . . . my wife and the mother of my children. I may have freed you from Newgate, my love, but I am imprisoning you once more. You are mine and never will you be free again!"

The joy on Allie's face as she comprehended his words was answer enough, and John Montgomery, Lord Norwich, wasted no time in sealing the fate of his willing prisoner.

# Reading—
## For The
## Fun Of It

Ask a teacher to define the most important skill for success and inevitably she will reply, "the ability to read."

But millions of young people never acquire that skill for the simple reason that they've never discovered the pleasures books bring.

That's why there's RIF—Reading is Fundamental. The nation's largest reading motivation program, RIF works with community groups to get youngsters into books and reading. RIF makes it possible for young people to have books that interest them, books they can choose and keep. And RIF involves young people in activities that make them want to read—**for the fun of it.**

The more children read, the more they learn, and the more they **want** to learn.

There are children in your community—maybe in your own home—who need RIF. For more information, write to:

**RIF**
Dept. BK-3
Box 23444
Washington, D.C.
20026

**Founded in 1966, RIF is a national, nonprofit organization with local projects run by volunteers in every state of the union.**

THIS SUPER-SELLER FROM
PAGEANT BOOKS WILL
CAPTURE YOUR
HEART!

Annie Ellis is a lady's maid in her mistress's clothing,
but the outfit is a wedding gown! Coerced into a
marriage meant for her mistress, Annie leaves
Chicago for the sandhills of Nebraska with her new
husband. Their hardworking days and sensuous
nights soon evolve into grand passion—but can
Annie shield the dangerous truth of her identity? Or will her new husband forsake her to shield
his wounded heart?

ISBN: 0-517-00623-5   Price: $3.95

AVAILABLE AT BOOKSTORES NOW!

# A NEW HISTORICAL ROMANCE FROM PAGEANT BOOKS!

## SAND CASTLES

### JEAN NASH

As a gorgeous widow in New York during the Gilded Age, Laura Sheridan never lacks for suitors, but she longs for passion and adventure, the kind she finds in the arms of Christopher Warren. As an architect, Warren is accepted as a gifted artist, but in society circles he is not an equal. Can his massive visions reshape even the unwritten moral codes of Fifth Avenue? Will Laura allow her growing love for this brash upstart to conquer her fears?

ISBN: 0-517-00061X    Price: $3.95

From the award-winning author of *Surrender the Heart.*